Margaret in Berlin

Also by R. L. Rhyse

Margaret of Greenwich - Margaret and Erika

Margaret at War - Margaret in Tokyo

Margaret and Eve - Margaret and Velda

Margaret and Emily - Margaret and Hillary

Margaret in London - Margaret at Barnard

Margaret at Barnard/Part Two: Deliverance

R. L. Rhyse

Margaret in Berlin
Book Twelve in the
Margaret of Greenwich® Series

Wyston Books, Inc.

Margaret in Berlin

Wyston Books, Inc.

www.margaretofgreenwich.com
www.wystonbooks.com

R. L. Rhyse
Margaret in Berlin: a novel
Book Twelve in the Margaret of Greenwich® Series
1. Margaret of Greenwich (Fictitious character)
2. Teenage Girls Fiction
Library of Congress Control Number: 2016915078
ISBN 978-0-9903920-8-8
eISBN 978-0-9903920-9-5

Cover Photograph by Rich Legg/
Licensed from Getty Images

BISAC: YAF022000 (Girls & Women)
YAF011000 (Coming of Age)
YAF029000 (Law & Crime)

There is the justice of lawyers and the courtroom,
and the justice of The Prophets and of God.
—Margaret

Margaret in Berlin

Margaret in Berlin

Chapter 1

Hacking into my medical record wouldn't be hard for my boyfriend, Randy. His computer professor at Yale had described him as "a genius."

And I trusted Randy with whatever he would learn. We had vowed to keep no secrets from each other though I held back a few. He's the nervous type.

Screams from my nightmares awoke my family for three consecutive nights and my father had insisted that I consult a doctor directly. This, though he had hesitated after suffering chest pains just weeks before. Being sixty-four, his symptoms were more than likely serious. At nineteen, mine indicated a recurring anxiety that I understood. They began three years earlier and the mind has its own schedule for forgetting.

But after consulting the doctor I worried that I had revealed too much. Mine hadn't been the usual teenage worries: about school, or a lover. Instead, I spoke of my kidnap and rescue by Spetsnaz (Russian Special Forces).

Ghosts from the City's murderous past had seemed to encompass me as I left the doctor's elegant office in Charlottenburg, a wealthy district of Berlin.

Chapter 2

Years before, when she was unusually upset, my baby sister had burst out, "I need a new family." But she hadn't been serious for we all loved her as much as any family members could. It had simply been a bad day for her, to put it mildly. Her therapist had been murdered, and in peaceful Greenwich, Connecticut too.

Here, in Berlin, I had just gained my unexpected *third* family. This household added to the adoptive parents who had raised me in place of my biological mother, Lena, and reputed English father, Peter. But I had recently learned that Vladimir, a former Russian general, might be my *real* biological father. Both men had been Lena's lover at the time that I was conceived. A DNA test was never performed and wouldn't be appropriate now.

This odd situation wasn't an issue since I loved both Peter and Vladimir and they loved me. I had gotten used to living in London over a previous summer and would now adjust to life in Berlin.

I wasn't sure how long I would be here. Barnard College's new term began in two weeks and I sensed that I wouldn't want to leave so quickly. Moreover, I had lied to my adoptive parents. I told them that I was returning to Manhattan early to visit a sick friend, not flying to Germany to meet my new father. I had felt that the truth would hurt them. Now, a phone call wouldn't be a good way to explain this mess that my lie had created.

So, like many with a seemingly insoluble problem, I put the issue out of my mind. It is only my second day in Berlin and I have time to decide, I told myself. I would go for a run and then find a café for breakfast. But I knew that the days were counting down and that I would eventually have to decide.

Chapter 3

That early morning, it was just after 7AM, I felt like a child does the first time they suspect that the man behind Father Christmas is their father. The child's part in that holiday game is to never speak their awareness of the truth. If nothing is said, the Santa pretense can be maintained.

This sounds like kindergarten stuff but the doctor said that it has real psychological value. "A person's life is easier if they can occasionally deceive themselves," he had told me.

I didn't know Berlin but had been told that it was a safe city. Even so, Vladimir had assigned an English-speaking bodyguard to accompany me on my explorations. She lived in the bedroom next to mine and had better hearing than my mother. By the time that I finished putting on sweats and sneakers, she was tapping on my door: treating me like a toddler whose baby monitor has alarmed. Which is what I asked her.

"There's no CCTV. You said yesterday that you run every morning at seven," Olga replied.

She seemed to be Russian, as are many of Vladimir's employees. Most are former soldiers or police officers. But she spoke German fluently, had lived in Berlin for years, and knew the City well. She would be a good guide and one can never be too well protected, I had told myself.

Olga had already advised me.

"Germany has a low crime rate but there are increasing incidents of violence. Be cautious at night, and never reach for money in public. I'd carry a walking stick too," she said.

Margaret in Berlin

Her last comment was accompanied by a knowing look. In London, a mugger had made the mistake of trying to rob me. I broke his nose and knee caps with the metal-tipped walking stick that I carried. Vladimir has probably told her this story, I thought.

Chapter 4

"Have you decided where to run?" Olga asked.

"In the street?" I answered casually.

Germany's customs weren't familiar to me. American drivers can be careless about runners and it might be the same here.

"I wouldn't recommend it. Germans are sticklers for rules, like not crossing the street against the light. We can run in the Tiergarten," Olga said.

"What's that?" I asked.

"A famous park not far from here. It's a former royal hunting grounds and touches on scenic buildings on every side. In the middle of the park is the Siegessaūle, a golden statue of winged-victory atop a column. I'll point out the sights as we run. Did you plan anything after running?"

"To wander a bit. Get to know the City and shop for rolls for the family," I replied.

"We'll take the car. The Park is ten kilometers away, that's about six miles. I'll name the streets to familiarize you with them," Olga said.

The car was a black Series 7 BMW sedan. Olga drove at high speed through the streets and I remarked at the car's great suspension. There was little body movement as we rounded corners.

"It's a wonderful car though the trunk is narrow and it takes time to learn the controls. The rear seat even has a multiple massage function for *mobilization, vitalization, and relaxation*. That's according to the manual," Olga said.

"I could use all of them," I said, with a smile.

She named the streets as we reached them.

"We're heading east on Behaimstrasse toward Wilmersdorfer. Soon we'll be crossing onto Richard Wagner Strasse and then turning right onto Otto-Suhr-Allee," Olga said.

She took the third exit at the roundabout. She parked a short time later, and we entered the park and began running.

Chapter 5

I was a consistent winner on my high school track team and tend to run at my personal pace. Slowly speeding to my fastest, then remaining there before relaxing to a walk. Others have their running style and, not knowing Olga's, I feared that her's would slow me. A bodyguard must remain with you, leaving her behind would be stupid, I told myself.

My concern was short-lived. Olga managed to keep up with me but I didn't go all-out. A runner's mind-set differs from a tourist's which is what I became as Olga pointed out the sights.

We began running at the west end of the Park, at Breitscheidplatz, past the ruins of the Kaiser Wilhelm Memorial Church which she said had been left in ruins as a reminder of the war. After picking up speed, other notable sights followed: the Zoo Palast Cinema, and the entrance to the City Zoo with its lion gates.

I slowed and then stopped after we crossed a footbridge over the Tiergarten Canal. The sight of the houseboats reminded me of Greenwich and my anxieties had left me. I felt calm and that I could sit there all day. Which is what I said.

"I understand but I have my orders," Olga said.

"What are they?"

"To show you the wonders of the City. Your father wants you to live here. You'll stay, won't you?" Olga asked, with a smile.

I thought for several moments. What about my life in Greenwich and study at Barnard? I asked myself. Decision time was arriving more quickly than I had expected.

Margaret in Berlin

"Let's go for breakfast. Where do you suggest?" I asked, with a smile, ignoring her question.

Chapter 6

"Chipps has the best vegetarian food in Berlin. How does that sound?" Olga asked.

"That would be fine. Did my father tell you that I was vegetarian?"

"Among other things," Olga admitted.

"He *really* needs you and wants you to stay," she said.

I nodded but ignored her implied question. Figuring out the best solution to my dilemma couldn't be made quickly.

"Chipps doesn't open until nine. We can relax here until then if you like," Olga suggested.

"OK," I replied.

Olga steered us toward a bench overlooking the canal. She remained watchful while I sprawled and closed my eyes.

"You've had a busy few days," Olga said, softly.

"You don't know the half of it," I replied, as my eyes remained closed.

I'm more worn-out than I realize, I told myself.

I knew nothing about Olga but sensed that we could be friends. Which was probably what my father intended. Having a close girlfriend in Berlin, even if she was his employee, would make remaining here easier for me.

"How was the flight?" Olga asked.

"It was a flight. There were no problems."

Margaret in Berlin

"Maggie, the woman that you met during your flight, has phoned your father. He's meeting her today."

I described Maggie's situation to Olga.

Maggie, whose birth-name was Margaret, had just resigned from the New York City Police Department. She did this after a tourist's video of her went viral. It showed her punching a reporter who had squeezed her ass. She was given the choice of resigning or accepting a demotion to street duty far from where she lived. She chose resignation and, being at loose ends, came to Berlin to visit her grandmother and flee her media infamy.

On the plane, I had told her of Vladimir's security company and suggested that she phone him about a job. He complains how hard it is to find good workers who speak English too.

"She's lost and needs a break. I hope he hires her," I said.

I heard Olga stretch and turned toward her. She was staring across the water though her eyes seemed unfocused. Finally, she spoke.

"That's what your father does. He gathers in and saves those who are lost, then sends them out to do battle," she said.

I didn't reply. Olga could have been describing me.

Chapter 7

We didn't speak more about Maggie or my father as Olga drove to the restaurant. She kept up her tour-guide commentary.

"Chipps is on Jägerstrasse in the heart of Berlin. It has panoramic windows that look out onto the lawn behind the Foreign Office. During warm weather, people eat on the terrace.

"The restaurant's centerpiece is an open show kitchen where diners can watch their dishes being prepared. The restaurant is popular with Americans since most of the waiters speak English," Olga said.

Her choice was a good one. Chipps' food was great and the service was quick and friendly. I gave the restaurant extra points for its free sourdough bread basket.

We had arrived just after it opened. The restaurant was quiet though it was probably busy at lunchtime and on weekends.

The breakfast specials had odd names. I chose the Sugar Daddy (pancakes, maple syrup, fruit salad), adding a croissant, muesli with cranberry-apple yoghurt, and orange juice.

Olga had the Lumber Jack (French toast, scrambled eggs, vegan bacon, maple syrup) and carrot juice.

While eating, my mind turned to my last hour in America. My best friend, Erika, looked distraught while saying goodbye at the airport but had brushed off my concern. I made a mental note to phone her after arriving in Berlin but had then forgotten.

Margaret in Berlin

My face expressed the anger that I felt toward myself and Olga noticed the change.

"What's wrong?" she asked.

"My best friend, Erika, looked upset when I left and I forgot to call her," I said.

"She probably worried about your flight," Olga said.

"No, she doesn't worry about little things," I said.

I took out my phone and dialed her number.

"Berlin time is six hours ahead. It'll be the middle of the night in America," Olga cautioned.

In my unease, I had forgotten this as the call went through. It would make no sense to hang-up now. Either I'll wake her up or my call will go to voicemail, I told myself.

But Erika was already awake.

"Where are you?" she screamed into my ear.

Chapter 8

I was so surprised by her angry tone that I didn't speak for several moments. Erika is the kind of person who stays cool during a crisis. Her mother and sister were raped and murdered when she was young and she's been seeing a shrink ever since.

Erika has always been my go-to girl on matters psychological. For her to scream "where are you," which she already knew, meant that she wasn't thinking clearly. Obviously, something big had happened or was about to. One of us had to remain calm.

"I'm in Berlin. I sensed that you were upset at the airport and meant to phone as soon as I arrived here. I'm sorry. What's going on?" I asked, softly, speaking slowly and deliberately.

"Clarence has diabetes. We were waiting for the test results when you left," Erika said.

Her voice sounded strangled but was under better control.

"OK," I said slowly, awaiting what she would say next.

"I can't live without him. I can't lose him."

"You're *not* going to lose him. Today, diabetes is treatable and even winning athletes have it. Sotomayor is diabetic too."

"Who's that?"

"A Supreme Court Justice."

"Yes, of course, I can't think. Clarence is shattered."

Margaret in Berlin

"Learning of one's serious medical condition does that but he's strong and will get over it. I did when I was a child and my condition was believed lethal."

Erika knew my story. I became *really* sick as a child and the doctors didn't know why. I couldn't concentrate and my grades went from "A" to "F." Finally, my parents took me to Johns Hopkins, which is possibly the best hospital in America. There, I was diagnosed as having Sanfilippo Disease. It's a genetic enzyme deficiency which makes the body unable to properly break down sugars. It leads to problems with behavior and attention, and children with this disorder usually died in their teens.

That I didn't die is thanks to the retired teacher who had been tutoring me while I was on home instruction. She was also a Santeria priestess and, during a dream, was "told" my cure: soybeans, which are sold in every health food store. I began eating them and my symptoms disappeared.

When I returned to Johns Hopkins, the doctors were astonished at my good health. They began researching soybeans as a cure, and may have already won a prize. So I know what it is to struggle with a serious illness, and Erika knew this.

"You're right. It's just the shock from learning it. When will you be back?" she asked.

"That's a story. Can I call you tonight?"

"*Anytime.* Don't worry about waking me. Stay well, sister."

We've long considered each other as sisters.

After I hung up, Olga, who had been trying to pretend that she wasn't listening, looked at me quizzically.

"Her fiancée just found out that he has diabetes. It's a shock. I'll call her back tonight," I explained.

"It's hard to be properly supportive," Olga said.

"That's not my toughest problem. Deciding where I'll be in two weeks is," I replied.

Chapter 9

I ate slowly. Chipps was so pleasant that I didn't want to leave. I watched the cooks work in the open-show kitchen and then stared out the panoramic windows. Nearby, teenagers listened to a mournful tune on an iPod. I moved my chair back from the table, sprawled and closed my eyes.

"It's *Wer hat dies Liedlein erdacht,* by Mahler," Olga said.

I softly tapped my foot along with the music.

"It's about a man calling for his love, a woman who would *make the young wise, the dead alive, and the sick recover*," Olga added.

I nodded as the silence between us became a comfortable one.

"I don't know what to do," I said, finally.

Olga said nothing.

"My adoptive parents, with whom I have lived for my entire life, believe that I'm in New York City with a sick friend and Vladimir, my biological father, expects me to stay with him. They're all good people and I don't see how I can avoid hurting someone," I said.

"Did you tell Vladimir that you would stay here?" Olga asked.

"Not in so many words. It was more implied since I've never lived with him."

The mournful tune repeated and deepened my mood.

"Do your adoptive parents know Vladimir?" Olga asked.

"Yes, but not that he's my biological father."

"OK. Why not spend your next semester studying at a German university? Many of our schools have programs in English and you could study German too. Maybe you could arrange to get credit for this so you could graduate from Barnard with your class. This way you could live with Vladimir and not hurt your adoptive parents. But how much to tell them is beyond my pay grade."

I considered her suggestion for several moments before speaking.

"That is a *genius* idea," I burst out.

"Now you know what your father pays me for," Olga said, with a smile.

Chapter 10

A few minutes later, Olga suggested that we leave and I agreed. As we reached the car, I remembered my intention to bring fresh bread home for the family. Buying bread in America is simple. One goes to the supermarket for the cellophane-wrapped brand that your family eats.

"Where can I buy bread?" I asked.

"At a bread store," Olga replied, in a puzzled tone.

"OK. Where is a bread store?" I asked, sinking into the leather-suede interior of the BMW as it glided along.

"Brotgarten was one of the first wholegrain bakeries when it opened forty years ago and is still one of the best. It sells twenty-nine different types of bread every day. Beside it is their small café where you can get vegetable soup and wholegrain Linzer Torte and apple cake," Olga said.

She hadn't exaggerated. Brotgarten was an abundance of buns, to use one of my terrible puns. The selection amazed me and would delight the heart of any foodie.

I gave Olga a wordless question and puzzled look.

"Let's taste," she suggested.

Olga spoke in rapid German to the sales clerk who gave us slices. All tasted wonderful, as different from American packaged bread as is the sun from the moon. I chose two loaves: Vollkorn-Saftkorn, a bread filled with seeds and grains that the clerk described as creating "a party in the mouth"; and Dinkel-Früchtebrot, a bread filled with fruits, nuts, and seeds.

After leaving the bakery, I felt the satisfaction that one gains after successful shopping. But my face had darkened by the time we reached the car.

"I'm still not sure what to tell my adoptive parents. Maybe I should ask Vladimir," I murmured to Olga.

"He won't tell you what to do. He'll review the problem and insist that you to decide. But you'll figure it out. Remember, life is a game and should be played with a smile," she said.

I nodded, and smiled as we entered the apartment.

Chapter 11

Even after his medical scare, Vladimir had continued with his usual work schedule. The only change was that he now did it mostly from his home-office. He had eaten breakfast earlier and Olga went to check in with him. I joined Ulrika and her baby daughter, Beauty. Her father's affectionate nickname had now become what everyone called her.

While sitting and watching Beauty, I snacked on Vollkorn-Saftkorn, the bread that the store clerk had described as being "a party in the mouth." It was.

"Could you stay with Beauty today? I have a medical appointment later and Vladimir has a formal dinner that we're attending this evening. He distrusts outsiders to watch her," Ulrika said.

"Of course. Babysitting is my job in America," I replied, with a smile.

I'm becoming part of my new family, I thought, feeling pleased but a bit uneasy. I still hadn't called my adoptive parents in Connecticut, or called back Erika, I reminded myself. Then I considered what Ulrika had just said.

"Is there a medical problem?" I asked, immediately feeling concern.

The ordeal from my father's Lyme disease and my childhood disorder had created lingering trauma about any doctor visit.

Ulrika looked uncomfortable, as if I had raised a touchy matter.

"If you'd rather not talk about it just tell me to shut up," I said, quickly.

"Well, it *would be* a bit early," she said, and, a moment later, "I may be pregnant."

"That's wonderful!" I exclaimed, with a big grin that she quickly joined.

"What's *pregnant*?" Beauty asked.

Olga looked stumped so I quickly chimed in. My expertise is coping with kids.

"*Pregnant* means that you're getting a sister or a brother," I said.

"I want a brother!" Beauty insisted.

"I think your daddy does too. I'll do my best," Ulrika said, softly.

"It'll be a big change. Two kids are much more work than one and for the both of you," I said.

"Yes, and your father isn't as young as he likes to think he is. I've long suggested that he reduces his schedule—become Chairman of the Board instead of running the company. Maybe now he will."

"I hope so. His heart attack scared me. Has he considered a replacement?" I asked.

Ulrika looked toward Beauty though there was no cause for concern. I sensed that she was unwilling to answer my question but she finally did.

"Yes, though they wouldn't have to begin work immediately. He has decided on *you*," she said.

Chapter 12

I stared at Ulrika.

"*Me? I'm* to run Vladimir's company?" I managed to sputter after several moments.

"Yes, *you*," she repeated, with a firm nod.

"But, but…"

I was still sputtering, feeling too surprised to speak yet certain that I should say something. After regaining my senses, I realized that Vladimir had likely asked Ulrika to test this idea with me, feeling that it go down easier if coming from a woman.

"Look, I appreciate the honor but I'm a college student. My fiancée and all of my friends are in America. Plus, I know nothing about management," I said.

"Vladimir won't fully retire for three or four years and will be around to advise you after that. You would have time to finish school and marry. Vladimir will tutor you and you'll learn what you need to know. Think of it as being an internship that your school would send you on.

"And you'd needn't worry about location. The company is international and opening offices in America. You would have the power to move its headquarters there, even to Greenwich if you wish."

I thought some more.

"But don't his two sons expect to inherit the business?" I asked.

"He's already spoken with them. They're happy being field agents and have no talent for management. You are family too and they know of your work in Japan and America."

Ulrika was referring to several of Vladimir's operations. The one in Tokyo had nearly gotten me killed.

It wasn't yet noon and my day had become impossibly complex. What should I tell Vladimir, what should I tell my parents, and how would I console Erika about her fiancée's diabetes? If all this could happen on my second day in Berlin, I dreaded the rest of my stay here.

"OK, I'll consider it," I said, hoping that Vladimir's idea had merely been a brainstorm that he would quickly forget.

"Do so! All who have worked with you are convinced that you are Vladimir's daughter," Ulrika said, firmly.

Her sons had already told me this but, when considering the activities that it had taken to earn their praise, many people wouldn't consider it a compliment.

Chapter 13

Beauty was delightful but, like most toddlers, I knew that she would need my total attention while babysitting her. I would have to make my phone calls before Ulrika left for her doctor's appointment.

I decided to call Erika first since she needed me the most. I would then call Randy. Even a long-term, faithful boyfriend needed regular checking-in with. The phone call to my parents I would save for last. It would be the most difficult since I still hadn't decided how to explain where I was.

"Well!" Erika stormed, to indicate that she had been awaiting my call.

"I'm sorry but things are blowing up here too," I said, apologetically.

"What's wrong? Is it Vladimir's health?" Erika asked, with an instantly changed, now concerned tone.

"No, he's fine. It's something else. I'll tell you later. How is Clarence?"

"He's adjusting to the diagnosis. He never got colds or anything else and had believed himself invincible. But now with diabetes..."

"It must have been a shock. Will he have to inject insulin?" I asked.

"He doesn't know yet. He's seeing the doctor tomorrow and I'm going with him."

I didn't know what to say and Erika continued.

"I read online about Justice Sotomayor. She was telling diabetic children about her experience. Her diabetes was diagnosed when she was seven. During her tests at the hospital, when a technician pulled out a needle to draw blood, she became so frightened that she ran from the room and out the hospital, hiding under a parked car. The staff had to drag her back, kicking and screaming, to finish the tests.

"She told the kids that learning to manage her diabetes gave her discipline, that while the disease was bad it wasn't *so* bad and that they should continue to do the things that they liked to do and to do them well.

"Nowadays, most diabetics can use an insulin pump but Sotomayor must inject herself four times a day, "Erika said.

"That's a good story for Clarence," I said.

"I plan to tell it to him. Now, what's the latest disaster in your life?" Erika asked, calmly, in her normal reassuring tone.

Chapter 14

"I don't know where to start," I said.

"Well like they say, begin at the beginning," Erika said.

"Briefly, my parents think that I'm visiting a sick friend in Manhattan, I gave Vladimir the impression that I would be staying with him in Berlin, and Ulrika just dropped the trial balloon that he wants me to manage his business. Not right away but after three or four years during which he'll tutor me. So who do I talk to and disappoint first?"

"Whew."

"Yes, whew."

"Do your parents know Vladimir?" Erika asked.

"They know him casually but not that he's my biological father. Everyone had believed that Peter is," I replied.

Our chat died for a few moments, neither of us having a good solution.

"What did you tell Ulrika?"

"That I'd consider it. Olga, one of my father's employees who has been acquainting me with Berlin, suggested that I attend a German university next term. If Barnard granted me credit for this, I still could graduate with my class. It would also push the manager decision down the road."

"That's a good idea but keeping a long-distance relationship with a boyfriend isn't easy."

"I know but I can't think of a better solution," I said.

"Have Randy join you."

"Huh?"

"He could study in Germany too. I read online that their tuition costs little. The country wants tech oriented youth and Randy is a genius with computers. His father is a cheapskate so Randy could use the excuse of wanting to save him the cost of Yale tuition and also to learn German to be able to read their research. Could Randy stay with you?"

"There are empty bedrooms so I don't see why not."

"That's too bad. He'd certainly prefer to share your's."

"That's an even better idea," I said.

Despite the gloomy sky, my day had suddenly brightened.

Chapter 15

I knew Randy's class schedule but because of the time difference between Germany and Connecticut I didn't think that I would get him in. The message that I left for him was brief: "Love you darling, just wanted to chat. Call me." This left me with my most difficult call to make, the one to my parents.

I knew that anything I said would hurt their feelings. How could I explain my being in Germany? It wasn't like you had told someone that you were going to the movies and went to the library instead.

But I lucked out. My parents weren't home and my fifteen-year-old sister, Melanie, picked up the phone. I wound up doing my usual: giving advice about high school drama though her latest worry had a potentially deadly twist.

Melanie's speech had a rushed, desperate quality, as if she had been awaiting my call. Or maybe for the call from any trusted older person that wasn't her parent. Some teenage matters aren't easily shared with them.

She was having a hard time getting started so I asked, "What's wrong?"

"What makes you think that something is wrong?" Melanie asked.

Her guilty tone caused me to remember what our lawyer-father had said: that a person who responds to a question with a question is either scared or about to lie.

"Because I love you and know you. Now, what's going on? Is it dad?" I asked.

I still worried though our father's health seemed to have fully recovered from his long struggle with Lyme disease, Randy had told me that I was a worrier and I am about the health of those that I love.

"I have a boyfriend," Melanie said, after taking an audible, deep breath.

"That's *great*," I said.

By tradition, Mormon teenagers don't engage in other than group dating until they're sixteen but our Mormon family is more flexible than many. I began dating Randy when I was thirteen, though we didn't call it that, and he isn't Mormon.

"Yes, well…" Melanie said.

She hesitated and I sensed that I wouldn't like what I was about to hear.

"He's nineteen and in the Marines. We had sex," Melanie confessed.

"Yes," I said, simply.

My tone expressed only that I had heard her, not that I approved.

"What's your question to me?" I asked, in a neutral tone.

"He wants to get married," Melanie said.

I suddenly felt afraid for her, and yet also a bit envious. Though being four years older, I was still a virgin.

Chapter 16

If there is ever a moment when an older sister becomes a parent this situation must be it, I told myself. There was no way that I would sympathize with, much less aid, any plan for her to marry now. But I also knew that saying this would be a waste of time. Love isn't controlled by logic. Thankfully, both I and Erika had been lucky enough to meet great boys before making the disastrous choice when the heart overrules the brain. What should I tell Melanie? I asked myself.

"I'm nearly sixteen and there are states where I could marry at sixteen, maybe even younger," Melanie said.

"Let me think for a minute," I said, hoping for clearer thinking from her.

An inspired idea from me would require more facts, I decided, and changed the focus of our conversation.

"Where did you meet him? How long have you known him? What's he like?" I asked.

I spoke these questions quickly, feeling that I would then be more likely to learn the truth rather than get the angry defiance that my immediate rejection of her idea would arouse.

"We met at the Mall a month ago."

"He comes from Greenwich?" I asked.

Though trying not to, I realized that I was beginning to sound like my mother would. And, though he was a lawyer who had heard everything, like my father would too.

"Yes, he's from the right social class," Melanie said, angrily.

"That doesn't interest me. I was afraid that he's one of those serial killers who roam the internet for beautiful girls like you," I said quickly.

I added the compliment to reduce the sting of what I had really said: that I hoped she hadn't been an idiot.

"*Right!* He asked if I wanted to see his puppy," Melanie burst out.

"Who are his parents?" I asked, ignoring her contempt.

I *was* sounding more like my mother. Next, I'd ask his financial prospects, I thought.

Melanie breathed deeply and the silence that followed indicated that she had made a decision. She would tell me everything, or at least what I needed to know to be able to give her good advice.

"His name is Mark. His dad is a partner in the accounting firm that sponsors the Day Care Center's yearly fund-raiser. He's Harry's accountant."

This fact changed everything. *Harry*, the nickname for *Hamilton*, is Erika's father who is one of Greenwich's local billionaires. If they were acquainted, there was no question about the standing of Mark's family. It might be crazy but it was certainly prosperous.

My sigh of relief was audible.

"Why did Mark join the Marines instead of going to college?" I asked.

"His father would only pay for college if he studied accounting. What would you have done?"

"Move to Germany," I said, before catching myself.

"*Huh?*"

"I'd do the same," I said quickly. "But look, you haven't known Mark long. Why not take some time and then decide? For couples to stick together they must be able to tolerate each other's idiosyncrasies. To consider *cute* what a stranger would consider annoying or even disgusting. You're both very young," I said.

I instantly regretted my final words since Mark was my age. But they didn't seem to matter.

"That's what I told him," Melanie said.

Her crisis was over for it hadn't been one. Melanie had just needed to share her secret with an older sister—who did keep secrets.

Chapter 17

"Is anyone else home?" I asked.

I wanted to complete my calls before my parents arrived home. I still hadn't decided how to explain my presence in Berlin.

"Claudine's home. Do you want to talk to her?"

"Yes, please."

Melanie screamed loudly, "Claudine, it's Margaret. She wants to talk to you." She then said to me: "Cassandra's battling the Mafia."

"Huh?"

"It's a video game, *Mafia III*. Different gangs are trying to bleed the Italian Mafia dry. Cassandra is the leader of the Haitian gang. Claudine loves it."

"Does mom know?"

"Of course not. Aunt Lena bought it for her on a shopping trip. It's a secret."

"I can keep secrets."

"Well, now you have two secrets to keep."

Claudine came on the phone a moment later. She too had been adopted, I as a newborn and she as a kindergartner. Being treated by my adoptive mother better than she did her biological children had first given me the thought that I might have been adopted. That, and because I am the only red-head in our extended family.

"What do you want?" was Claudine's unenthusiastic response.

"Just to say 'hello.'"

"Hello."

"I get it, you're busy. I just want to say that I love you and miss you," I said.

My voice was more emotional than I intended and Claudine picked this up. Though very young, she is no dummy.

"Are you alright?" she asked, with concern.

"Yes, I'm fine. Just checking in with everyone."

"You don't sound fine."

"School can do that to you. How is your school going?" I asked quickly, wanting to turn the conversation from me.

There was a momentary silence while Claudine considered this.

"OK. Why doesn't mom like Aunt Lena?" she asked suddenly.

This issue had troubled me for years until I figured it out. Our mother's anger toward Lena, her sister, was not because she had left the Mormon religion to adopt her husbands' religions. Her first husband was Evangelical Protestant and her second husband was Jewish.

Nor did our mother's feeling derive from jealousy of Lena's business success and wealth. It was because she feared that Lena would wean my affection away since Lena is my biological mother.

But this would never happen. A person's parents are those who loved and cared for them as they developed, not those whose genes they inherited. Both I and Lena recognized this but my adoptive mother never would. I didn't know if Claudine was old enough to understand but I would try to explain, briefly. When seeking an explanation, kids want only a sentence or two, I reminded myself.

"Lena is my biological mother and this can make things...sticky," I said.

"Hmm...can I go back to my game?" was Claudine's response.

"Yes, love, see you," I said.

Melanie came back on the phone.

"Have you ever been to a topless beach?" she asked.

That question shocked me.

"No. Why?" I asked, answering her question with mine.

"Just wondering," came the vague response.

Her reply caused me to wonder too.

Chapter 18

Babysitting Beauty presented no problems. She did her own thing, which is what three-year-olds do. She fed her (stuffed) baby bear and then took him for a ride in a toy truck. Then she listened closely as I read to her from a Disney book, *When is Later. It* began, fittingly enough, with the sentence, "The baby-sitter had just brought Baby Mickey and Baby Minnie back from a long ride in their wagon."

The story was in English and Beauty understood. Vladimir is firm that she become fluent in English. "It's the business language of the world," he told Ulrika. This made my babysitting task easier since I had learned only a few German phrases since arriving in Berlin.

Olga joined us a few minutes later. My life seemed at loose ends. I had no plan for after Ulrika returned. What would I do the next day and the next? I didn't know.

In Greenwich and Manhattan, I had roots and friends. Here, I had a new father, a new step-mother, and a new half-sister. I also had a tour guide. Olga, who served as my bodyguard too though Vladimir hadn't yet told me why he felt that I needed one.

The two thousand Euros and DKB Visa credit card that he gave me I did understand. Everyone needs money and the card was hooked into an internet checking account if I needed more. Vladimir trusts me.

Olga held the hand puppet of a baby dinosaur and sat beside Beauty. The dinosaur's head kept hitting against the head of Beauty's stuffed bear.

"Friends shouldn't fight," I cautioned.

"Not fighting, kissing," Beauty corrected me.

Obviously, her mood was better than mine.

I silently watched them play and soon noticed a change in Olga's face. Was it sadness? Longing? I didn't know.

"Do you have children?" I impulsively asked Olga, though not knowing why.

Olga kept playing as if she hadn't heard me.

When she did respond, I didn't know what to make of her answer.

"I don't know. I really don't know," she said softly.

Chapter 19

While Beauty played with Olga, I tried to make sense of what she had just said. How could a woman not know if she had children? I could understand this of a man after a barely remembered one-night stand but not of any woman. She had either given birth or not. There could be no question about it.

My puzzled look aroused Olga's response. Indicating Beauty, she said, "I'll tell you later."

Later, was after Ulrika arrived home with the exciting news that she was pregnant. Beauty danced with joy and we were all smiles.

To celebrate, the maid brought coffee, juice, and the Dinkel-Früchtebrot bread that I had bought. It is even better toasted.

Ulrika turned toward me.

"I'd like you being with me when I give birth," she said.

She had referred, indirectly, to Vladimir's desire that I remain in Berlin.

"I feel torn in two. I want to be here and in America too. Olga suggested that both I and Randy, my boyfriend, spend our next semester at a German university. Could he live here too? I'd feel better. We plan to marry but..."

"You trust him, but..." Ulrika said, with a smile.

"Exactly."

"We have plenty of space. Have you asked him?"

"Not yet, I wanted to run it by you first. I still haven't decided what to tell my parents in Greenwich," I said.

"I'll speak with Vladimir. He's been handling tricky situations all his life and may have a suggestion. I'll see him after my nap. It's been a long day for me, and he'll have other news to digest too." Ulrika said.

With that, she left the room.

Beauty was taking the stuffed bear for a ride on a toy truck in a distant corner of the large room. I watched her for a minute before turning toward Olga.

"How can you not know if you're a mother?" I asked.

Chapter 20

Olga looked away. When she finally spoke it was as if she were talking to herself, reliving some long-past terrible event that she feared to revisit.

"I had twins but was never their mother. They were taken from me immediately after their birth and I never saw them again."

I looked toward Beauty. She was still engrossed with her play. Olga's story would be *some* story and I hoped that it wouldn't be interrupted. She took a sip of coffee and this seemed to bring her back to the present.

Olga stared into my face.

"I owe Vladimir my life," she said.

I nodded. Months before, at a wedding celebration in Manhattan, I had met a Russian diplomat. Vladimir had saved his life too, while both were soldiers in Afghanistan.

Olga's story was shocking, but not for me. Claudine, my baby sister, had an equally horrible experience before my Greenwich parents adopted her.

"Both of my parents are doctors but they don't practice medicine. They're bureaucrats of the Council of Europe. They write regulations to ensure the quality and safe use of medicines throughout Europe, helping member nations to avoid repetition of work and unnecessary costs. Their task isn't well-known publicly but is one of the Council's more important ones."

Olga's inward stare returned and I waited for her to continue. When she didn't, I asked the most non-threatening question that I could think of.

"What country did they work out of?"

"France, in Strasbourg which borders on Germany. It faces the River Rhine and the German town of Kehl. Strasbourg had a bad air pollution problem from heavy industry when I was growing up but this got better over the years."

I nodded to indicate that I was listening. Beauty was still busy. She and her bear friend were having a long talk.

"Strasbourg has a history of pogroms, wars, and natural disasters. Why it was chosen as the seat of the Council of Europe has always puzzled me. I left as soon as I could."

"Where did you go?" I asked.

"Back to Berlin, which has its own disastrous history. But I grew up there and it was home. I chose Humboldt University, to study math which I was always good at.

"I didn't have a place to live when I arrived and stayed at the University's guest house. That was where my parents said goodbye, and from where I vanished without a trace."

Chapter 21

I looked toward Beauty just at the moment when she squealed. Everything had looked to be going fine but I knew that a toddler could amuse themselves for only a short time. She had probably reached it.

"I'll be back in a minute," I said, touching Olga's hand.

It took more than a minute. I asked Beauty what was wrong and she replied that her friend was hungry again. I brought the bear a slice of bread, watched for a while, and left Beauty's side when she was again fully engaged.

"She'll be OK for a while," I said, after returning to Olga's side.

Now, Olga continued her story as if she hadn't been interrupted. Her voice had a haunted quality and I sensed that she had long yearned to examine her experience. A traumatic event can do that even many years later. But Vladimir had assigned Olga as my guide *and* bodyguard so he had faith in her strength, I reminded myself. What could have happened to her? I wondered, as she spoke in an anxious tone.

"If you like, we can go to *The Barn* tomorrow. It's a student hangout and during my first week at university I spent every evening there. They have wonderful homemade carrot cake with cream cheese frosting and sandwiches on flaky croissants. They also have the best single origin coffee, from micro-roasters like Denmark's Coffee Collective. But I'm sure that they have juice too," she added, remembering that, like most Mormons, I don't drink coffee.

"That would be *great*," I agreed, wanting to move her story along.

Olga nodded and made a brief smile that wasn't a real smile.

"I spent every evening at The Barn," she repeated. "I had never lived away from home and felt free for the first time. Probably like you did when you went away to college."

I smiled and nodded again though I had felt more terror than freedom at Barnard. My parents had always allowed their children the freedom to explore. My fear came from the possibility that I would get lousy grades and lose my scholarship. This would have made it impossible for me to attend college and working as a waitress didn't appeal to me.

"The Barn was where I met Rudolf," Olga said, as her eyes took on a vacant quality.

I hesitated to explore this obviously upsetting matter but curiosity reigned. After a minute, when she didn't continue, I asked, softly, "Who is Rudolf?"

"Who *was* he, you mean."

Though puzzled, I nodded and waited.

"Rudolf was my first lover but the day that he dies will be the happiest day of my life. I don't expect to see my children again. But if I do and if they're well, it wouldn't be fair to drag them from the only family that they've known after all this time," Olga said.

Though her tone was defiant, as if expecting an argument, I had none to give. I had already learned that there exist human monsters who are undeserving of life. Though still not knowing what had happened to her, I said what I felt and hoped that it would help.

"I've been there too," I said, and my tears evidenced that this was true.

Chapter 22

Now Olga stared. Several years before, while working for Vladimir in Tokyo, I had barely avoided death through torture at the hands of a monster. I would have joyously killed him but this was done by others.

"I had considered our meeting a casual pickup but was wrong. I was selected and our meeting had been planned. He had wanted a young woman from an upper-class background like mine. She need also be highly intelligent and healthy. There could be no genetic defects or history of insanity in the family. Being tall and blond were important for this order; other people made other demands. Creating a blond child for a Saudi prince wouldn't do."

Olga had probably felt free to speak openly because she had recognized that, despite our differences, we had both suffered greatly. My being Vladimir's daughter also helped.

"My parents tell me that I shouldn't blame myself. After all, I had just turned eighteen and how worldly can any teenager be. But I should have trusted my instincts. There were times with Rudolf when I felt uneasy but I had pushed these feelings away. I told myself that I was grown up and could take care of myself, that I had traveled with my parents and met all manner of people. Moreover, one shouldn't be rude and hurt someone's feelings. God, was I dumb."

I understood for I had behaved similarly and known others who had made this mistake too. Humans still possess a reptilian survival instinct and ignore its warnings at their peril. Despite this, I still had no idea what Olga was talking about and told her.

"I don't understand. Exactly what is it that happened?" I asked.

But a moment later, in a flash of insight, all that she had told me came together and I did understand.

"You were kidnapped and impregnated and forced to bear a child," I exclaimed.

"Yes, and not one child but two. Those monsters got a bonus: two healthy, made-to-order children to sell," Olga said.

Chapter 23

Olga's story now flowed. The Barn had been crowded when Rudolf sat at her table. He claimed to be a student too and they bonded over his tales of university life. He had told her only a few personal details: that he was born in Hamburg, and was studying medicine. He had seemed more interested in her and who doesn't prefer to talk about themselves?

That her parents were doctors gave them another element in common and it soon felt like she had known him for years. They even loved the same movies: the rawness and intensity of Fassbinder's *The Marriage of Maria Braun*, and the fear-ridden, claustrophobia of Petersen's *Das Boot*.

His approach had been relaxed. There was no quick invitation to his apartment, not even to a darkened movie theatre where she might fear that intimacy would be pressured. In short, he did all the right things to reassure her of his honorable intentions.

"I liked him and he took advantage of me," Olga said.

"Many girls can say that," I observed.

But I knew that my statement provided no comfort. The only remedy for dumb behavior is to learn from the experience.

I checked to see how Beauty was doing: she was still busy. The rest of Olga's story was bleak. Early one evening, while leaving The Barn to go to the university for classes, Rudolf said that he had forgotten a book and they went to his apartment to get it. Once inside, she had been Tasered, gagged, and tied with duct tape. When it was dark, she was carried to a waiting van and driven to a house containing a medical setup. She had been told what would happen and that she would live only if she cooperated. If not, she would be of no value to them and would be killed.

She would not be raped or harmed since this would affect the baby that she would be carrying. Rudolf promised that she would be released after giving birth.

"Did you try to escape?" I asked.

"I once did but never again after I saw what happened to another girl who tried," Olga said.

Beauty's scream filled the room when her teddy bear fell from the toy truck on which she was taking him for a ride. I looked over but she was OK. She seemed to be developing a melodramatic streak. I sipped juice and awaited the rest of Olga's story.

Chapter 24

"My room had been set up like a hospital room and wasn't uncomfortable. It had a TV and its own bathroom with a shower. Meals were brought in and I was told that whatever books or magazines I wanted would be provided. The room was in the basement and the door was locked with a deadbolt. There was no lock on the bathroom door but no one ever entered when I was using it. Once a week I was taken to another room while my room was being cleaned but I never saw the person doing this.

"I had no idea where I was or even if I were still in Germany. Once in the van, I had been given an injection and quickly fell asleep. It might have been many hours before I was awakened by the vibration from a rough road. A few minutes later we reached the house where I was kept prisoner.

"I tried to keep calm, knowing that panic was my worst enemy. They had to keep me alive until I gave birth. There would be time for me to plan my escape.

"I didn't know how many people were in the house. I had seen three: Rudolf; an older, fit man in his forties; and a woman in her thirties who was described as my doctor. She spoke good German but with an accent, maybe Slavic. There might have been a cook but I never saw them. The walls were thick so I never heard any sound apart from those that I made.

"About two weeks after I arrived, the door to my room was accidentally left unlocked. The doctor had been giving me a daily fertility injection and she got a call on her phone. She had left the room while speaking on it and without locking the door.

Margaret in Berlin

"I waited for a few minutes before opening the door. Then, carrying my sneakers, I tiptoed up the stairs, listening before taking each step. The basement door was open and I saw no one around. After reaching the first floor, I noticed a windowed door leading outside. I left the house and moved quickly toward the shelter of the trees and brush. I had nearly reached it when the earth in front of me burst upward from a bullet striking it."

Chapter 25

Olga became silent, lost in memories and gazing into her coffee cup. She sipped for several minutes before I asked, "What happened then?"

Olga looked up suddenly with a terrified expression and then resumed her story.

"I turned, Rudolf motioned with his pistol, and I walked back into the house and down into my basement cell. Before locking the door, he spoke softly. 'Your foolish behavior almost got you killed. This is your last chance,' he said.

"After that, things continued the same as they had been: daily fertility injections which left me feeling bloated; re-reading magazines; eating food which was considered nutritious. I learned that other girls were there from the voices and crying that I heard when my door was briefly opened and they passed it.

"One day, Rudolf took me from my room into the one farthest down the corridor. It was furnished similarly to mine. There, a girl of about my age stood on a stool. Her hands were tied behind her and there was a rope around her neck hanging from a hook in the ceiling. She looked...terrified.

"Rudolf turned toward me. 'She tried to escape,' he said. When he nodded, the man standing by the stool kicked it away and I was forced to watch while she strangled."

I waited and said nothing. There was nothing that I could say.

"I closed my eyes, trying not to hear her choking, and fainted. When I came to I was laying on my bed. Rudolf sat on a chair reading. When he saw that I had regained consciousness he said, 'She was no loss. She couldn't conceive.' Then he slammed shut the book that he was holding and left the room.

"I understood his warning. I had been forcing myself to vomit, trying to avoid becoming pregnant. If I can't conceive, they'll have to let me go, I had mistakenly decided. Rudolf had showed me that I was wrong.

"So I began cooperating. I no longer complained about the side effects from the fertility injections and followed the doctor's instructions to the letter. When I became pregnant, they congratulated me that I would have twins. As my due date approached, I was moved from the house."

Chapter 26

"A scarf was wrapped around my eyes during the move but I wasn't restrained in any way. I was in a delicate condition and they probably feared to harm the babies. And being very pregnant, I was in no condition to flee.

"When the car stopped, the blindfold was removed and I was taken through the rear door of a hospital to a service elevator. Once in my room, I was given the usual procedures before delivery: an enema and pubic shave. Rudolf watched everything and you would have thought that I would be embarrassed but I wasn't. No man except a doctor had seen me naked since I was a baby and that was my father. But being a prisoner takes away all sense of shame or embarrassment.

"Then I was placed on a bed and an IV and fetal monitor were hooked up. There was a nurse and a man who I assumed was a doctor. He gave me instructions in what sounded like a Slavic language and Rudolf interpreted.

"There were problems during the delivery but not big ones. The umbilical cord was wrapped around one baby's body, and there was a slight tear in my perineum, the area between the anus and the vagina. The doctor explained that this was common during a first childbirth and said that it would heal on its own without stitches.

"The water bag was broken to speed up labor. It went quickly and I was glad of this. Rudolf didn't want me given a painkiller for fear of harming the babies. Like I said, I didn't count. I was simply their bearer.

"After delivery, the doctor showed me my sons and smiled. The nurse cleaned and wrapped them and took them to the nursery for their first bath and exam. Then the doctor spoke and everyone left the room. He seemed to have said that I needed rest and Rudolf didn't object. I had the sense that the doctor and nurse weren't criminals, that Rudolf had told them he was my husband and that we were traveling and had found ourselves here. While in the car, a wedding ring had been placed on my finger.

"Despite Rudolf's promise, I was sure that he wouldn't allow me to live. Why would he? I knew what he looked like and has witnessed a murder. The punishment is the same for one killing or two.

"I decided that I would have only once chance to escape and it was then. I dressed quickly, waited a minute to give them time to get the babies to the nursery, and then slipped from the room. I ran down three flights of stairs, out the rear door and through the parking lot. I didn't know the local language or where I was. I just ran."

Chapter 27

I didn't need to encourage Olga to continue her story. Her anxious tone told me that nothing except knocking her out could have stopped her.

"I didn't know how much time I had before they discovered that I was gone. But where should I go? After leaving the parking lot I ran through a copse of trees and uncut brush. I crawled through a slotted fence and continued running but now more slowly, not wanting to trip and break something. I raised my legs higher though sensing that the bleeding from my perineum tear had not yet stopped.

"When I was out of breath, I fell onto the ground and listened. I could hear voices in the distance but couldn't make them out. The luminous dial of my watch said that it was 9:14PM. Darkening clouds shielded the moon. It'll soon rain and I must find shelter, I told myself. I was worn out and wanted to sleep but fear kept me awake. I had to find shelter, a phone, anything!

"I closed my eyes and prayed. It was something that I hadn't done since childhood. My family wasn't religious and my parents hadn't been in a church since their wedding. 'Lord, let me die quickly. And if there is a Heaven, let my parents and brothers join me someday. On, onward to Zion,' I prayed, though also thinking that I'd gone a bit crazy. But when I raised myself, I could hardly believe what I saw. There, in the distance, was a light. It was faint but was definitely a light.

"I got up from the ground and began walking toward it but slowed as I grew closer. Could this be one of Rudolf's tricks? I wondered.

"The light was inside a barn. I stood frozen and unsure what to do. Was Rudolf inside? Fear of being murdered had paralyzed me for months and I had just endured childbirth. I had reached my limit of endurance. I entered the barn. In the dimness, I saw an axe with a broken handle by the door. I grasped it and hefted its weight.

"I raised the axe and walked slowly and quietly. The light had come from a stall in the rear. The barn lacked the smell of a working farm. It had probably been deserted for years. If Rudolf found me, there would be more deaths than mine, I vowed. I would not be killed without difficulty.

"The stall's door was open and I slipped inside. My steps were soundless on the straw. Upon hearing movement, I tightened my grip on the axe. Then I heard a scream."

Chapter 28

"It was just teenagers having sex. I understood why the girl screamed. I must have looked like something out of a horror movie: a creature with matted hair and clothes stained with mud and blood holding an axe. The scream pulled me back to my senses. Explain with a simpler story than the truth, I told myself.

"I dropped the axe and asked, in three languages, if they understood German or Russian or English. My family is tri-lingual. The girl understood German and I explained.

"'I was raped and held prisoner. I am trying to get away and need help,' I burst out. They stared for a moment and then hustled into their clothes.

"'We'll help you,' the girl said, without asking any questions. No one should ever say that teenagers can't be brave! 'Is he close?' the boy asked.

"I don't know."

"We'll take you with us. I have an ATV. Come!"

His tandem four-wheeler wasn't intended for more than two passengers but we squeezed on. He drove, I sat in the middle, and the girl clung to us. He seemed to know the trail well because it was only when we were far along that he turned on the headlight. After a few more minutes of travel, he stopped and turned toward me.

"Do you want to go to the police?" he asked.

"Where are we?" I asked.

"Just outside Pilsen."

"In the Czech Republic?"

"Yes."

I thought quickly. Except for these two, I could trust no one. The police might be corrupt and bribed to return me to Rudolf. And if they were honest, they would certainly detain me since I lacked proof of identity.

"No, not the police. Can you drop me somewhere safe from where I can be picked up?" I asked.

"St. Bartholomew's Cathedral is always open and everyone knows it," the girl suggested.

"That would be great. Is it far from your homes?" I asked.

Though it was too dark for me to see, I sensed the boy's grin as he spoke.

"No, and taking you there would be our pleasure. We don't often get the opportunity to be heroes. But don't say a word to the priest about where we met. We'll keep your secret too." the boy said.

"We parted with hugs and an exchange of phone numbers. I'll repay them someday, I vowed.

"The priest was German. I told him that I had been raped and didn't want the police involved. I needed to call my parents. He gave me a phone and food and water. The church is eight-hundred-years old and he hid me in the underground tunnel beneath it. I phoned my parents. They thought that I was dead.

"I insisted that they not call the police. I didn't want to become a TV sensation that I would never live down. 'Let the world believe that I am dead,' I told them. So they phoned

Margaret in Berlin

Vladimir who sent bodyguards and a doctor. I was brought to this apartment and it was here that I was reborn."

Chapter 29

Beauty had become antsy. She was tired of playing alone even if the teddy bear was her best friend. So I played along with them for a while, while Olga composed herself. For a moment, as she spoke of her narrow escape, she had no longer seemed the confident martial arts expert/bodyguard that I knew her to be. She had been shaken and looked vulnerable. I returned to her side and awaited more of her story.

"I couldn't face my parents after what happened. They had looked forward to having grandchildren. But I felt screwed up sexually and didn't want to bear more children. And besides, what had become of the children that I had?

"My mind wasn't operating rationally. I was getting flashbacks and nightmares. The doctor that Vladimir sent me to called it Post-Traumatic Stress Disorder. I was depressed and just wanted to curl up in bed and die.

"Vladimir helped me to find a future. He said that after something bad happened, one can either give up or fight and become strong and that which path I took was up to me. I chose to be strong.

"I lived in his apartment for a year. After several more days of moping around, Vladimir said that work would save me. I began doing little things, filing and making copies in his office. One day he asked me to read a report and tell him what I thought. I said that I thought its conclusion was wrong and told him why. He agreed and said that he was promoting me to his assistant. I would answer the phone and field general questions.

"After three months of doing this, when I no longer felt afraid to be alone, Vladimir said that I was very young and asked what I hoped to do. I told him that only two things could return me to life: finding my sons, and killing Rudolf."

Olga paused to sip coffee.

"Was Vladimir shocked? "I asked.

"No. He nodded approval and said, 'Then you have work to do. When battling a despicable enemy, the nastiest person will win.' The next day I legally changed my name to Olga. The girl that I had been no longer existed. My cozy past life was over."

Chapter 30

"'Fit youngsters have amazing powers of recuperation. You'll enter the fiery furnace a girl but will leave it a heroine,' Vladimir told me, and that was my intent. Though not to be a star but to become strong, and to find my sons.

"If I find them quickly, I'll bring them home though their father would have equal rights, I thought. And the parents might be innocent, paying for the services of a surrogate mother but not knowing of the criminal acts.

"But if this takes time, and my sons are much older when I find them, would it be reasonable to rip them from the only parents that they had known in order to satisfy my need? Vladimir discouraged my worry. 'When you find them, you'll know what to do,' he advised me, and I still believe that he is correct.

"But I had other worries too. I was never a *physical* person. Reading, not sports, was my interest. Now, to achieve my goals, I had to enter a different world. Soldiers understand this and I think that you do too."

I nodded. Though I had been a track star, the dirty survival tricks that I learned aren't taught in any high school.

"Where were you trained?" I asked.

"Not far from here, on the outskirts of Berlin. Vladimir's company has a training camp for new recruits. It's run by former Spetsnaz (Russian Special Forces). Some of their exercises are insane."

"Like what?" I asked.

"To do almost physically impossible things: flip over a barbed wire fence while accurately throwing a hatchet. But

Margaret in Berlin

Vladimir supervised my training closely. He had no interest in my learning showy things. He ordered my instructors to condition me physically, and to teach me Krav Maga."

Chapter 31

Now I had two questions. The first was why she had taken the name, Olga, and the second was what Krav Maga is.

"Why did you choose Olga? What is Krav Maga?" I asked.

Olga looked toward Beauty, implying that her explanation would take more than a few words. I looked too. Having fed her stuffed bear friend, Beauty and he were napping arm-in-arm.

"It was Vladimir's idea. Olga was the name of his daughter," Olga said.

This was news to me. I hadn't known that Vladimir had a grown daughter. I had learned only months before how he had gained the scar on his neck—but this fact had come from his wartime comrade. I wondered how much more about Vladimir's life I didn't know. Was he purposely keeping painful events from me?

"I didn't know that he had a grown daughter," I said.

"He doesn't. She was killed in a Moscow terrorist bombing when she was seven. The historic Olga ruled a Russian state in the 10th century after the death of her husband. Maybe Vladimir felt this name would fit. My presence would lessen his feeling of loss, and suggest that I could be powerful too," Olga said, and I nodded.

"And Krav Maga?" I asked.

"Krav Maga is Hebrew for *contact combat* and is considered the most advanced form of self-defense. It emphasizes the need to identify threats before an attack occurs, but also to avoid violence whenever possible. Boxing and wrestling aren't brutal enough for street combat. Krav Maga has adopted elements from all of the martial arts techniques. It has three basic ideas: to attack or counterattack quickly to the body's most vulnerable points such as the eyes and groin; to seek objects that can be used for defense or attack; and, while dealing with the threat, to look for escape routes.

"It sounds like you don't need any more than that," I said, feeling impressed.

"That's not true. You don't take a knife to a gun fight," Olga said.

It was a good "line" but didn't belong to her. Ulrika had said this in Tokyo, when she trained me how to kill.

Chapter 32

Beauty awoke and my conversation with Olga ended though I still had another question. She was now twenty-seven-years old. What had she been doing since recovering her health? But this answer would be for another day since just then one of Vladimir's secretaries entered the room. Vladimir wanted to see me *now*.

A body's first reaction to fear can be many things: feeling hot or cold; getting a pounding heart rate, dry mouth, or sweating; even, and I've heard soldiers report this unashamedly, soiling themselves. None of these events is disgraceful. Machines function as they usually do no matter what but people are not machines.

Though Vladimir loved me he could still make me nervous. I had seen his employees quake when confronting his anger—and these were seasoned ex-soldiers who would terrify anyone.

While walking to his home-office, I considered why I was nervous. If he were annoyed with me and yelled, I would simply listen and think through what he had said. If agreeing with him, I would apologize. If not, I would argue the facts and ignore the heated emotion. My lawyer-father in Greenwich advises this technique and I had always found it to work best.

I knocked on the door before entering. Vladimir lay on the sofa with his head upraised on pillows and folders on the floor. He looked relaxed and not angry.

"Ulrika told me that you have a problem," he said, in a caring tone.

"Which one?" I asked.

Margaret in Berlin

I had wanted to give myself time to think but instantly regretted what I had said since it sounded disrespectful.

Vladimir thought for a moment before answering, in a calm tone.

"The problem with your adoptive parents in Greenwich. They appear not to know that you're here."

"Yes, I lied to them," I said.

"Please pardon me if I'm intruding. Soldiers aren't good at dealing with emotional matters," he said.

I sensed with surprise that, at that moment, Vladimir seemed as nervous as me. An employee who knew Vladimir well had once told me that Vladimir likes for others to view him as being easy-going and friendly but that he had been a high-ranking military officer too long for this to be possible.

"I asked Ulrika to speak with you about it but she said that was my role," Vladimir said.

I wanted to make the discussion easier for both of us.

"I planned to speak with you but got talking with Olga. I don't know how to tell them that I'm in Berlin and not Manhattan as they believe," I said.

I had deliberately referred to my adoptive parents as "them." As I have explained, my family is complicated.

"I have an idea. Why not return to Greenwich and tell them that you've been offered a scholarship to attend a German university for the next term. I'll put you on our payroll. You can do some work for us and invite your boyfriend to do the same. Your parents need never know that you lied though I *would* tell your father and he can inform your mother. She seemed high-strung when I met her."

"That's a *great* idea," I said.

Vladimir beamed and I rushed to hug him. What he suggested had been the plan that *I* had thought up before our meeting, but parents feel more secure if believing that an idea is really theirs.

Chapter 33

When you want things to move quickly, they often don't. Flying home was no simple matter. I had already missed several flights that day and most of the others had two stops. I finally settled on an SAS flight leaving Berlin at 4:25PM and having just one layover in Copenhagen.

I would arrive at Newark Airport at 9:05PM, take a shuttle bus into Manhattan and then the train from Grand Central Station. Once in Greenwich, I would take a taxi home. Arriving so late would awaken my family and their joy at seeing me would make tough questions less likely. But I felt guilty for this isn't how one should behave with those who love you.

I packed quickly, kissed everyone goodbye, and promised to return carrying a surprise present for Beauty. Olga drove me to Tegel Airport and waited until I boarded the plane. We hugged and my last words to her were, "I want to know more," and she understood. We had already achieved a measure of closeness so that I didn't have to spell it out.

Tegel Airport was as it always is. Small, jam-packed with people, confusing, and considered by many to be the worst airport in the world. Security is so strict that one person complained of being nearly sexually assaulted by a guard operating an electronic scanner. This didn't happen to me. Maybe because I smiled.

The flight to Copenhagen was on a Canadair RJ900. The seat cushioning was minimal and I felt as if I were sitting on a hard plastic shell. There was no Wi-Fi or in-seat power. The best that can be said of the flight is that it lasted only fifty-five minutes.

I had never been to Copenhagen and would have liked to see the city but the layover was one-and-one-quarter hours so this wasn't possible: the airline terminal is on an island, five miles south of the city.

I hadn't eaten and was hungry. Having only a few minutes before boarding, I decided that the best thing to do would be to get take-on food. Since there was no time to study menus, I quickly decided on pizza.

At a restaurant called *Gorm's*, I bought a Margherita. It was described as being "The Mother of All Pizzas": tomato, mozzarella, and basil. All acceptable ingredients for my vegetarian nature.

"There are only two ways to live: being a victim or being a fighter and you must decide which you want to be," I heard the man in back of me tell his companion.

I almost jumped from déjà vu, the sense of having experienced something previously though it is really only the first time. These words were almost exactly what both what my Greenwich father and Vladimir had told *me*.

Chapter 34

"No matter how striking the conversation, it's rude to eavesdrop," my mother often says. But, being nosy, I continued to listen.

The accent was British, the kind that you hear from BBC news reporters.

"You must decide for yourself but you know what your mother would have wanted you to do," the man continued.

Then came a muffled sob and sniffling and the sound of a pocket opening.

"Here," the man said.

He had apparently handed something, a handkerchief or tissues.

There was a long queue for take-out at Gorm's and I was fourth in line. Intrigued by the conversation in back of me, I purposefully dropped the paperback that I held. While turning to pick it up, I saw the people who were speaking. They were a prosperous looking middle-aged man wearing a three-piece suit and a young woman carrying a twenty-three-hundred-dollar snakeskin bag by Miu Miu. My best friend, Erika, whose father is a billionaire, also owns this bag.

As they continued speaking, I slowly understood the situation. The woman was married to a man who beat her. He owned guns and had threatened to kill her if she left him.

My lawyer-father had said that for an abused wife to rely on the court for protection in such a situation is often more dangerous than doing nothing. The woman was traveling to America, to live with her aunt and begin a new life. But she was "paralyzed with fear," she said.

Margaret in Berlin

The man who spoke was her father. The story that he told her reassured me and I planned to tell it to others. It is a Buddhist fable, and was allegedly written by Buddha himself.

Two thousand years ago, a beautiful white elephant was captured and given to the king. The king turned her over to his elephant trainers to be taught to follow commands. They were harsh and beat the elephant severely. One day, crazed by pain, she broke free and ran away.

The elephant ran fast and outdistanced the trainers who pursued her. Finally, they returned home and the elephant was free. Yet she was unable to forget that she had once been captive. She would run at full speed when hearing any noise, as from the rustle of leaves or a twig snapping.

A tree spirit could tolerate seeing the elephant's pain no longer. He whispered in the elephant's ear: "Do not fear the wind for it moves only the clouds and dries the dew. You must look into your mind for it is fear that has captured you."

Then the elephant realized that her fear came from her habit of being afraid, and she began enjoying life again.

There was a moment of silence after the man stopped speaking. Then I heard the rustle of clothes as child and father embraced, and he said softly, "My baby."

I felt like hugging him too.

Chapter 35

Upon boarding the airplane, I saw a cart set up in front of the first row. I needn't have bothered bringing water since it contained juice, water, Champagne, and newspapers.

I'm tall and appreciated the ton of legroom that the seats had. Each pair of seats was in its own fixed pod so that when you reclined, the seat moved forward and down rather than into the person behind you. When fully reclined, you were only a few inches above the floor which felt odd. So I relaxed with the seat mostly reclined but not in the full flat mode position.

On each seat was an amenity kit containing ear plugs, a water bottle, and toothbrush and toothpaste. The ear plugs were effective in blocking out the engine noise while I napped.

The plane didn't have an in-flight entertainment system. Instead, there was an iPad containing some movies and a few episodes of TV shows. Not all of the iPads had the same movies so one could ask to swap for another tablet. There was also a fold-down screen showing the aircraft's current position.

I had allowed the woman from the airline terminal to board the plane ahead of me. The Business Class cabin had four seats in a row with two abreast. The plane was crowded and, given the choice of sitting next to her or a suddenly leering man, my choice was obvious.

"Do you mind if I sit here?" I asked politely.

This really isn't necessary for one doesn't own the seat beside them. But whatever courtesy I lacked after my Greenwich mother's upbringing, my London grandmother had drilled into me.

The woman didn't reply. She removed the Gorm's food bag from the seat beside her and I occupied it. Her eyes were still red from weeping.

I decided to wait until the woman began eating before beginning to eat. That could give me the conversation opener that we had both purchased food from the same restaurant. I would point to my bag and ask how her food choice was. Teenagers are instinctively cunning.

After making the usual announcements, the flight stewardess came around with information about the upcoming meals and offer of drinks. I declined and the woman asked for "an Airborn."

When the stewardess left, I asked the woman, "What's an Airborn?"

She didn't bother turning but did reply.

"It's a mixture of vodka, cognac, and ginger ale," she said.

The plane took off, the seat belt sign was extinguished, and her drink arrived.

I sipped from my juice box, she gulped her Airborn, and then opened her take-on bag. I glanced over. It contained pizza with sliced pepperoni. I opened my food bag, lifted a slice of my vegetarian pizza, and took a bite. After swallowing, I turned toward her.

"This isn't as good as the pizza that you can get in New York's Little Italy," I said.

She ignored my statement and continued eating. When not looking down at her food, she looked out the window. I finished eating.

"That was good. I was hungry," I said, brightly.

Then I did what dopey kids sometimes do though with a different purpose. I "accidentally" squeezed my juice box too hard and a few drops squirted onto her skirt.

"I'm sorry," I said, with excessive feigned embarrassment. "What a thing to happen. I'll pay for the cleaning. That's enough to ruin a day."

"Screw it. It's just one more in a life filled with cock-up's," the woman replied, irritably.

Then she began crying.

Chapter 36

Despite her pained expression, if I hadn't lived in London for a summer I might not have understood what she had said. Simply put, a *cock-up* doesn't refer to the male organ but is a mistake that one has made. *Screw it* means that one should forget what happened and move on, an attitude which few would argue with. This attitude, and being nosy, define me according to my mother and she is right.

No matter what someone has said or how they look, it is easy to mistakenly assume that they want our advice. We often tell them what to think or ought to do when what they really want is a friend to listen and, with this, to regain their strength.

Despite this, it's hard not to offer help in some way though this can cause the helper to fall into the same hole as their friend.

After numerous such mistakes, I had accepted that the best thing for a friend to do is to offer understanding. This fosters hope and keeps the person on their feet a bit longer, until they grow tough enough to fight another round. Moreover, the friend that you save today will be stronger when you need their help.

The woman wiped her eyes and finished her pizza. She ordered another Airborn when the stewardess came around.

After the drink arrived, the woman took a sip, turned toward me, and introduced herself.

"I'm Pamela," she said, with the glimpse of a smile.

"Margaret," I replied, with a real smile.

Margaret in Berlin

Then Pamela took another sip of her drink, relaxed in her seat, and began speaking. Thus did our friendship begin.

"I sometimes think that my life is a huge cosmic joke, but one so far above me that I can't understand it," she said.

I understood her pain. Every person's life might have once been shattered had something had gone differently. Or might still be destroyed if fate goes against them. Many will love you when you are successful but far fewer when you are not. I try to be different. So I listened as Pamela shared her pain, and then I shared my pain too.

It is routine to speak freely of personal matters during travel. The strangers that one meets remain strangers and are never seen again. This is what I assumed would happen that day. But fate had another intention.

Chapter 37

I remained silent, waiting for Pamela to continue as I had behaved earlier with Olga that day. Today will be filled hearing the stories of agonizing experiences like many from my own life, I had thought. Yet, unlike most of my childhood, Pamela's family must be prosperous as judged by her clothing. But Olga's family was well-off too. I reminded myself that wealth can ease a life but not insure it against tragedy.

Pamela's story of her marriage was so common as to be nearly a cliché. Her father is a high-ranking official of the British government. While accompanying him to Denmark on business, she had met a "beautiful man."

He was fifteen years older, a corporate lawyer, and owned a seaside house. She fell in love with him and her father had approved their union after checking out his family. This, despite the great age difference. "My mother died when I was young and my father was all that I had. Maybe I needed another father-figure," Pamela told me.

The wedding ceremony had been a fairy-tale with a horse-driven carriage and all. The honeymoon ended three weeks later when her husband's loving behavior suddenly changed.

One morning he became angered by something that she had done. It was a tiny matter and she no longer remembered what it had been. He slapped her hard on the ass and she screamed but didn't object. She interpreted his action as being playful, even sexy. But his behavior soon became extreme.

After a day at work, he would drink, throw things, and beat her. She wanted to go to college but he rejected this idea, describing her as being "stupid and worthless." After a while she believed this. He slowly took over her life: telling her what to wear, taking away her phone and passport, and keeping her a virtual prisoner in their country home which was overseen by an elderly housekeeper.

When she told him that she wanted a divorce, he refused and said that he would sooner see her dead. On some evenings, when he was *really* drunk, he played Russian roulette: pointed a six-shot revolver loaded with one bullet at her and pulled the trigger. Now, terror froze her in place.

One morning, after he had left for work, she went to the top-floor of the house to end her miserable existence. She intended to throw herself from the balcony onto the rocks below.

Then, she believed, "God intervened" through the ringing of a phone.

Chapter 38

I had almost stopped breathing when Pamela reached this point in her story. But her narrative was interrupted by the arrival of a stewardess who offered us the latest issue of *Allure*. This "Skin Care Issue" advised "What Dermatologists Use on Themselves." We passed on the offer.

"The ringing came from a cell phone in a jacket that had been left out to be taken to the cleaners. I called my father and told him what had been going on. My husband hadn't allowed me to contact him since our marriage. My father was shocked. The English aren't emotional but he screamed on the phone. He arranged for a British diplomat in Copenhagen to bring me from the house to the airport, by force if necessary. He met me there and here I am."

At that point, dinner was served. Pamela chose the fried cod with olive oil mashed potatoes, mixed vegetables, and a seafood salad. She remarked that the food was over-seasoned but OK. Her tone had become normal.

I chose the ricotta cannelloni with creamed spinach, grilled peppers and tomato sauce. It was a decent vegetarian option. The pasta was chewy but the filling was flavorful, average airline food.

"You're lucky to be alive," I said, as we finished eating.

"I certainly am. His first wife wasn't as fortunate. They never found her body and he may have killed other women too," Pamela said.

When we look back in our lives, we recognize a moment when we moved in a new direction. The change may be the result of planning or accidental but there is no turning back.

Margaret in Berlin

The moment may be just that: a look is exchanged or a sentence is spoken. It may be after a weekend or a month when the issue is in doubt until this change occurs.

For me it was after hearing Pamela's story that I recognized my mission in life: to provide safety for people's lives. I was Vladimir's daughter and would someday manage his security business. Now there would be no turning back. I didn't know how my intention would mesh with Randy's dreams but we would work it out. I had accepted my fate and was content.

Chapter 39

"What do you plan to do now?" I asked Pamela.

"I'm not sure. I'm too thrilled with the idea of being alive to have made plans. I'll just stay with my aunt and explore the City for a while. I'd like to go to uni. I always wanted to be an engineer. Would you believe that?"

Uni is British slang for *university* or *college*. Do the people here really speak English? I sometimes asked myself during my summer in London.

It was hard for me to visualize Pamela in other than her elegant clothes.

"Muddy work boots at all?" I asked, with a smile.

"Muddy work boots and all," she replied, returning my smile, which was now real.

"Are you a student," Pamela asked.

"Do I look it?" I replied.

I wasn't trying to be flip but to give myself time to think. How much did I want to reveal to her? Then I apologized for my less than friendly tone.

"I'm sorry but it's been a hard day though better than yours. I'm in my second year at Barnard. If I can arrange it, I'll attend school next semester in Berlin where my father lives."

"Your parents are divorced?" Pamela asked, making the logical leap of thought.

"No, it's more complicated than that. I was adopted by an American couple at birth and grew up in Greenwich, Connecticut. That's a short train ride from New York City. I recently learned that my biological father lives in Berlin. I just visited with him and want to know him better so I decided to study there for a while."

"How exciting."

"I'm lucky since I've heard that these meetings don't often go well. But I've known him for years though not that he was my father," I said.

"Do you know your biological mother?"

"Yes, but for most of my life I believed that she was my aunt. Like I said, it's complicated."

A look of sadness passed over Pamela's face.

"I wish that I had my mother," she said.

I simply nodded for there was nothing for me to say.

"What kind of work does your father in Berlin do?" Pamela asked.

"He's a retired Russian general and owns a security company,"

"He's Russian?"

It was the usual response that I get when a person learns this.

"Yes, but his partners are retired from the CIA and Britain's Secret Intelligence Service. Their business is international."

"He sounds *brilliant!*" Pamela said.

Brilliant is British slang for *great*.

"He is, and I love him very much," I replied.

Pamela stared as I choked-up with emotion. But I wasn't ashamed.

Chapter 40

We didn't speak again for several minutes. But this was the comfortable silence that happens with good friends, which is what I sensed we were becoming. Meanwhile, we both had much to consider. My future discussion with Randy, and what Pamela would do with her life.

I have one older sister. Pamela might become another, I thought.

"Are you sisters?" came a young voice from above.

A small girl peered over her seat, ignoring her mother's attempt to pull her back. I turned and smiled at the mother's nervous apology.

"It's fine. Flying is boring and it's always good to make a new friend," I said.

The child beamed.

"I'm five," she said.

"I have a sister who is a little older than you," I replied.

"I'm Dallas. What's her name?"

"Claudine."

"That's a nice name."

"So is Dallas," I said.

Our conversation petered out and the child returned to her seat.

"You have a way with kids," Pamela said.

"I should. I did babysitting for years in Greenwich and still do it in Manhattan." I said.

"I never have. I wonder what it's like being a mother, a *real* mother."

"Endless work and little appreciation. My next business will be selling the kids of worn-out mothers," I burst out. Then, at Pamela's shocked expression, I added, "Just kidding. I do love kids, at least most of the time."

People tend to relax when they are eating and to be nervous when they are flying. This may be why airline attendants keep pushing refreshments. To keep travelers from considering the fragility of humans as they hurtle through the sky.

We cooperated with the appetizer cart. I had salmon spread with crispbread and fennel salad. Pamela had crackers lain with ham with goat cheese.

Then, as if to reinforce a decision that she had made, she said to me, "No more Airborns."

Being Mormon, I don't drink alcohol or coffee or tea but I also don't try to impose my life style onto others. What they choose to do is fine so long as they allow me that freedom too.

Pamela leaned back and closed her eyes. As the plane was landing, she spoke again,

"My husband vowed to kill me. What do I do if he finds me?" she asked.

Her calm that had existed during the recent hours was gone. Pamela's fear was back.

Margaret in Berlin

My answer began as the plane touched down. It continued at Newark Airport, where I had last been just two days before.

Chapter 41

"I overheard the advice that your father gave you: to be either a victim or a fighter," I said.

Pamela's reply was to hand me a clipping from a British newspaper. It told of four women in Berlin that had been identified. They had survived abuse in the home of a couple that was suspected of having killed two other women. A forty-six-year-old man and forty-seven-year-old woman were placed in custody after calling an ambulance for a woman with head injuries. She died in the hospital and doctors had alerted the authorities to signs of abuse.

"OK, but that doesn't change what your dad said," I stated, after reading the article.

"No, but my danger is real. My husband has vowed to kill me if I left him. He's a monster."

After our plane landed, I steered us toward the restaurant that was now familiar to me. Before my departure flight from Newark, I had read many window menus seeking vegetarian food. The Café Flora's selections came closest.

My years of babysitting had taught me that downplaying a child's fear doesn't work. They simply feel that you don't understand what they have said. What does work is to tell them a relevant story from your life. One showing how you successfully dealt with what they confront or fear that they will. So that's what I did with Pamela. And that the event happened in her hometown was an advantage too.

"I was mugged in London last summer," I began.

"Were you hurt?"

"Not quite," I said slowly, exaggerating the words and adding a wry smile.

"Huh?"

"I was carrying a heavy, metal-tipped walking stick and smashed his nose with it. Then I broke his kneecaps, to put him out of business for a while."

"What did the police do?" Pamela asked, after a long stare.

"Nothing since I ran home before they arrived. I was about to return to America and didn't want to have to remain in London as a witness. And though he had threatened me with a knife, they might not have approved of all my actions."

Pamela said nothing as she considered this. I continued speaking.

"I'm not downplaying your danger. My best friend, Erika, has had a bodyguard for years. That was since her mother and sister were raped and murdered. There are real dangers in the world and you must trust the reptilian survival instincts that every human has. Flee whenever you sense danger and don't worry about being considered rude!"

We exchanged phone numbers during the taxi ride to Manhattan.

"Call me anytime. I know people who can help. Do you want to stay with me in my Barnard dorm for a few days? Your husband would never find you there."

"No, that would be an imposition and my aunt's apartment has a doorman. I'll be safe there," Pamela said.

"Remember, call me!" I emphasized, as she was leaving the taxi on East Sixty-Seventh Street.

"OK, but I'm sure that I won't have to though I do want us to keep in touch," Pamela replied, with a smile.

As soon as the taxi pulled back into traffic, my thoughts returned to *my* worries: the sticky conversations that I must have with my parents and with Randy. I moped in the dorm for three days until gaining the courage to travel to Greenwich.

There, at the door, it was—joy! We hugged until my older sister, Melody, grabbed me away to tell me about her latest Tinder dating disaster.

"He said that he was a writer and had reviewed *Zootopia*. Have you seen it?"

"No," I replied.

"It's animated and sounds like a kid's movie but you'll love it!" Melody gushed.

She has a degree from New York University's Film School and her life goal is to be a movie critic.

"Hmm," I said, being unsure where her story was going.

"I Googled his name to find the review and the first hit was a property record. He and his wife just bought a new house and he has three gorgeous kids. As I was looking, he messaged me to ask for a second date. I never unmatched someone so fast."

Melody is into online dating.

Just then my phone twittered. I excused myself, placed it to my ear, and heard Pamela's frantic voice.

"I'm in a restaurant bathroom. My husband has found me. He's threatened to kill me if I don't go home with him," she burst out.

Margaret in Berlin

There are thousands of people in New York City who could better help Pamela, I told myself. But she had called me.

Chapter 42

"OK," I said.

I had spoken slowly and deliberately. At that moment, Pamela would have to gain her strength from me.

"Take two deep breaths and tell me where the restaurant is," I said.

Her panting slowed. She was obviously in the grips of an anxiety attack.

"It's on First Avenue and Ninetieth Street."

I thought quickly.

"Is the bathroom a single? Is the door locked?" I asked.

"Yes, I'll check the door."

I heard slight sounds before she returned.

"Yes, I did lock it," Pamela said.

"Very good. Does the restaurant have a rear exit from which you can leave without your husband seeing you?"

"Yes, I saw it. But I left my purse on the table and don't have money!"

"Don't worry about that. I must phone someone but will call you back within two minutes. Don't move from the room!"

"I won't! I won't!"

I hung up and fished a business card from my wallet. Men criticize how many things women carry but it's usually not they who have to deal with emergencies.

Margaret in Berlin

I dialed the number. It picked up on the second ring.

"It's Vladimir's daughter, Margaret. I need your help with an emergency," I said, speaking quickly but clearly too.

"It would be my pleasure to serve you," came the immediate reply.

Piotr had given me his card when we met at a wedding reception months before. Decades earlier, when both were soldiers, Vladimir had saved his life in Afghanistan.

"My friend is being stalked by her murderous ex-husband. She is hiding in a restaurant's bathroom nearby. Could you provide her a safe haven for two hours, just until I can arrange for a car to pick her up?"

The silence that followed aroused my worry. My request was not modest. It could have major political repercussions.

"Her father is a high ranking British official. He is Permanent Secretary of their Treasury Department," I added.

This response came quickly.

"The Russian Federation would be pleased to provide a humanitarian service to Her Majesty's government. Would you like me to send guards to escort her here?"

"No, she's highly strung now and that could freak her out. She'll be there in five minutes."

"She will be admitted immediately. What is her name?"

I told him.

"Give my best wishes to your father," Piotr said.

I promised that I would, thanked him, hung up, and phoned Pamela.

"The address that you're going to is at 9 East 91st Street. In front of the building is a narrow area enclosed by an iron fence. This leads to a gate that is opened and shut after each person is permitted entry. You will be admitted instantly but may have to go through a metal detector."

"What is it?" Pamela asked, with a note of hesitation.

"It's the diplomatic mission of the Russian Federation. The Consul-General owes my father a favor and you'll be safe there. I'll send a car to bring you to Greenwich. Your husband will never find you there. *Go now!*"

I hung up immediately to avoid her arguing or second thoughts. Then I phoned Erika.

Chapter 43

Erika began speaking before I could say a word.

"I have mono, the kissing disease, though that's not mostly how it spreads," she said.

Erika sounded happy, not ill, and that's what I told her.

"I *am* sick. I can barely walk to the toilet. But I get over things quickly and should be OK in a few weeks. And being sick gets my dad home early, to have dinner together in my room."

"There's an emergency and I need a favor," I said, breaking in.

"Anything," Erika replied, turning serious.

"A woman that I met on the plane, Pamela, is escaping from her murderous husband. I arranged for her to hide at a safe house in Manhattan. Can you have her picked up to stay with you for a few days until things get sorted out. Her father is a British Treasury official," I said, speaking in a rush.

"Give me the address and I'll send Abram. It's his day off and he's probably in his room."

I told her the address.

"It's the Russian Federation's diplomatic mission. The Consul General's name is Piotr. He's an old friend of Vladimir. It might be best if Abram took an SUV," I said.

"It's that bad?"

"It could be."

Her family's SUVs are armored and carry machine pistols in a compartment under the seats.

"Can you stay over? I'm longing for company and you'll be safe if you keep your distance," Erika asked, pleadingly.

"I can't stay but I'll come for a while. I need to have sticky talks with my parents, and with Randy too. Have Abram pick me up at home. I'll go with him to Manhattan," I said.

Then, as an afterthought, I added, "Pamela is our age and really nice."

"But made a bad mistake in choosing a man."

"She isn't the first girl," I said, before hanging up.

Then I felt guilty at the insinuation. *Her* fiancée, Clarence, was definitely not a bad choice.

Abram arrived at my house twenty minutes later. He complimented my mother as he usually does and it took effort to pull him away from her suggested cookies and talk. Converting people to the Mormon faith, even an avowed atheist like Abram, is her serious sideline. He smiled, apologized that we were in a rush, and took the cookies with us.

Outside, I noticed that Abram had brought someone with him. Oleg sat waiting in the driver's seat. He was another bodyguard. Obviously, Erika had accepted my warning.

Chapter 44

The travel time from Greenwich to Manhattan can be between one and two hours depending on the traffic. That day it took a little over an hour.

Five minutes after leaving my house, our car merged onto I-95 and entered New York State. I had often traveled this route. At the traffic sign indicating I-287 West, I closed my eyes and began worrying. I dreaded the upcoming conversations with my parents and with Randy but neither could be avoided. If growing up involves becoming better at coping with difficulties, I would learn a lot today, I told myself. Then I dozed off.

Upon opening my eyes, I saw that we had entered the Henry Hudson Parkway. The Consulate was just a few minutes away and I remembered what I should have done earlier: informed Vladimir of what was happening.

He picked up on the second ring and I began speaking immediately, relating the situation as briefly as possible.

"I've arranged for a woman to temporarily hide-out at the Russian Consulate in New York. Her husband abused her and may be a murderer. Her father is the Permanent Secretary of Britain's Treasury Department. Abram and Oleg and I are traveling into Manhattan to pick her up. She'll stay at Erika's house until other arrangements can be made.

"I'm sorry that I didn't ask your permission first but there was no time. She called me from a restaurant's bathroom while her husband waited in the dining room."

Though being an adult, at that moment I felt like a child who might have misbehaved and now risked their parent's anger. Or a very junior worker confronting the company's CEO.

"Piotr has already called to express his nation's gratitude. He invites you to dine with him—and to meet his unmarried grandson!

"You did well. Considering the West's economic boycott, Russia will gain a valued friend in the British Treasury and our company has gained another friend in Her Majesty's Government. But your behavior reveals something personal too."

"What's that?" I asked, feeling puzzled.

"In making this decision, you have shown your strength as a manager and chosen your career," Vladimir said.

It took several moments for the impact of what Vladimir had said to fully sink in. Then, when it did, I nodded to myself.

"Yes...I have," I said slowly.

Chapter 45

As our car passed 102nd Street, I phoned Piotr to inform him that we would arrive in five minutes. Parking was, as is usual in Manhattan, impossible to find so Oleg remained double-parked outside the Consulate while Abram and I entered.

The iron gate was quickly opened. Pamela and Piotr stood inside the door, flanked by two obvious security men. Before we left, Pamela shook Piotr's hand. He kissed mine and extended the dinner invitation at his apartment.

"Come to Moscow. There, we will show you a *real* party," he said, and I smiled.

The Russians are an emotional people.

Once the car was moving, I told Pamela what had been arranged.

"Erika and her father will be pleased to have you as a guest for as long as you wish. They have a huge house and my father's company provides security comparable to that of the White House. You'll be completely safe. Your husband could never reach you," I said.

Pamela didn't reply. She simply began crying.

"How can I repay you? I have no money," she said, as she dried her eyes.

"You owe nothing. Friends do favors for friends. Someday I may call upon you," I said.

Then I mentally kicked myself for that line was straight out of the gangster movie classic, *The Godfather*. But Pamela was too worn out to notice. She nodded, leaned back and, with an exhausted sigh, fell asleep. I woke her gently when Erika's house came into view.

The housekeeper, who had apparently been informed, greeted Pamela effusively by name and led us upstairs. Erika was sitting up in bed.

"I have mono. Don't come closer!" she yelled, as we entered.

The housekeeper left. Pamela and I stood in the doorway and Erika looked at Pamela.

"Make yourself at home. Your bedroom is next to mine and you'll find the usual hotel stuff in the bathroom. The Wi-Fi password is beside the iPad, and feel free to phone anywhere. Once you're settled, Abram will take you shopping for what you need," Erika said,

Erika was Greenwich High School's most civically active student. Organizing comes naturally to her.

"But I have no money. I left my purse in the restaurant when I fled my husband," Pamela said, in an embarrassed tone.

"*Don't worry about that*. We have charge accounts in most stores. You're our guest and everything is on us," Erika replied, with her warmest smile.

I couldn't help smiling too. Like me, Erika was the budding manager of her father's business. His hedge fund holds worldwide investments and has an office in London. Friends do favors for friends and having the Permanent Secretary of the British Treasury owe him a favor would be a valuable asset.

Chapter 46

Abram drove me home once Pamela settled in. Erika had invited me to stay for dinner but accepting the invitation would strain my mother's patience. One of her rigidly enforced commandments is that, except for a medical emergency, the entire family eats at 6PM.

My father's increasingly busy law practice since recovering from Lyme disease had already upset her routine. He had begun arriving home late and, considering the touchy issue that I planned to raise, I was reluctant to miss dinner. But Erika understood. We had been as close as sisters for years.

My dad got home late again but it was only ten minutes. He washed up, joined us, and our family's usual friendly bickering began.

Our dinners aren't quiet. Problems or events are raised for discussion and we all chime in. It's a happy family and I hesitated to rock the boat until Melanie, my fifteen-year-old sister, gave me a perfect opening.

"There's a school trip to Germany next month, to meet other tech-minded students. We'll live with German families near a college in Berlin. The school has arranged for a cheap airfare and our living expenses will be paid by a foundation. I'd love to go," she pleaded.

I could have kissed her. The Lord works in wondrous ways, I thought, not for the first time in my life.

Surprisingly, neither of my parents looked upset. I wouldn't have expected this from my ordinarily calm father but my high-strung mother's lack of unease was surprising. Attending the parenting group at our Mormon Church is obviously helping her, I thought. I risked speaking my two cents.

"Many Mormon missionaries live abroad for years," I said casually, as if apropos of nothing.

My mother couldn't refute this argument. Her attempts to convert others to our faith are continual. But she does so courteously and her wonderful cookies make the experience at least a culinary treat.

Our dad gave Melanie the parental blessing.

"We can afford the airfare now and an allowance too. It'll be a great educational experience," he said.

I waited until all had resumed eating.

"I've considered studying in Berlin too," I said.

Chapter 47

My parents could hardly refuse me permission to study in Europe too. I was four years older than Melanie and would be living in the same city. So they agreed but with conditions: that I would monitor her behavior, whatever that meant, and that we would Skype with them daily.

I said that Vladimir's wife was pregnant and that they had offered me a live-in job as babysitter. This was close enough to the truth that I felt only a little guilt. I *would be* living with Vladimir's family and did *occasionally* babysit Beauty.

Though my parents had looked serious, the rest of us were all smiles. The excitement rose as I described Vladimir's apartment.

But I had spoken carelessly and seemed to know too much. After dinner, my father took me aside to his home office. He motioned for me to sit, sat back in his favored recliner, and looked at me expectantly.

"Tell me about it," he said, giving me his no-nonsense lawyerly stare. So I told him everything: my learning of Vladimir's heart attack, and that he is my biological father; of my flight to Berlin and lie that I was in Manhattan; Vladimir's desire that I manage his security business when I completed college and my aiding Pamela; and my anxiety about talking to Randy.

Then I waited, feeling nervous but unafraid. I knew that my father loved me and trusted his judgment.

"I understand," he said simply.

My father rose from his chair, spread his arms, and I rushed into his embrace.

"You'll do great things," he murmured, almost in benediction.

"I'll never hurt you or mom," I promised.

"You haven't told us all that happened in London and Tokyo, have you?" he asked.

"No, but I didn't want you or mom to worry. I was well protected in those cities," I said, as tears entered my eyes.

"You must be a very special girl for so many people to love you. But it's long past time that your mother and I learned whatever you feel we should know. We trust our children and allow them their secrets. It would be best if you told us together," he said.

We went to my parents' room. There, I described my terrifying experiences in London and Tokyo, but took care to emphasize that I turned out safe and sound.

Chapter 48

During my absence from home, my sisters' problems had built up. They mobbed me after I left my parents' room, seeking my sisterly wisdom.

Melanie's worry was typical and concerned her eighth grade prom, I suggested; "It's more important to focus on the memories than your hair. Take lots of pictures."

But seven-year-old Claudine's problem surprised me for it concerned her "boyfriend."

"I love Gerald but we never talk because we both get so nervous. What can I do? Or should I wait for him to talk first?"

Well, maybe seven-year-old isn't so young nowadays, I told myself. One of my friends had kissed her first boy when she was five and later spoke of him as being her "first ex." I took Claudine's question seriously.

"Talk to him what you talk with other friends about: teachers or movies or food. You can also ask friendly questions. What does he think of his teacher or life in Greenwich? You can also ask for help with something. Boys like to think that they're better," I suggested.

When my sisters left, feeling satisfied with my advice, I thought of calling Randy. But, still being unsure what to say, I decided to ask Erika. Thanks to her years of therapy, she had become my trusted adviser about relationships.

My father let me use his new car. It was the latest reincarnation of the Chevy Camaro that he had loved as a teenager. Driving this speedster removed my mind from my problem until the flashing colored lights in the rear-view mirror gave me a new one.

Margaret in Berlin

"You disappointment me, Margaret. You were doing forty-four in a thirty-mile-an-hour zone," the policeman said.

I've met many police officers in Greenwich through a family friend, Sergeant Alamo. He babysat me for years.

"I'm *really* sorry. I was worried about things and probably imagined myself on the highway," I said.

My tone *was* worried for I *was*. My parents insist that their children being law-abiding and I always had. Except for good causes, that is. My obvious shame and his knowing me worked the magic.

"I'll let you go with a warning but don't speed again. I don't want to have to pull you from a wreck," he said.

"You won't and thanks, really. My parents would kill me if I got a ticket," I said.

"Well, maybe not quite that," came his reply, with a smile.

I suddenly remembered that his wife's name was Nina and that they had five children with the youngest still a toddler.

"Give my regards to Nina," I said, returning his smile.

He drove off and I didn't drive above thirty-miles-an-hour that evening.

Chapter 49

Erika was sitting up in bed when I entered her room. I took my place on the chaise lounge, which was at least fifteen feet from her. Catching mononucleosis was the last thing that I needed.

"How do you feel?" I asked.

"A little better each day. There's no treatment for mono. Antibiotics don't work against viral infections so the only medical advice is to get good nutrition and plenty of fluids and bedrest. It'll leave at its own pace," Erika said.

"Can I do anything for you?" I asked.

"Yes," Erika said, and tossed me the envelope that lay beside her.

"Type them a note saying that, regrettably, I won't be able to help this year. Add that I appreciate the good work that they are doing and enclosing my contribution," she said.

On a Saturday in each May, Greenwich has a Town Party at the Roger Sherman Baldwin Park. While music by well-known groups dominates the event, there are also the usual food, face-painting, and family activities.

Though the party is on town property, it is not a public event. It is funded through a non-profit organization that needs community support to keep the festival affordable for all residents.

The party helps local social service agencies spread the word about what they do, raise money, and attract volunteers. It's not a small affair: eight-thousand people attended the last party that I attended.

I sat at her desk and got busy typing on her laptop.

"Toss me my checkbook. It's in the top left-hand drawer." Erika said.

Erika approved the letter and placed it and a check in the envelope that I had addressed. I returned to the chaise lounge.

"How is Pamela doing?" I asked.

"She's exhausted and went to bed right after dinner. She hasn't yet called her father," Erika replied.

"She probably doesn't know what to say. Having made a calamitous marriage and now the stalking."

"Communication can be a bitch," Erika mused.

Her statement pushed what had lingered in my mind to center stage.

"I've got a problem. A big one," I said.

At this, Erika perked up and her face glowed with interest. Solving problems is one of her many talents.

I continued speaking without waiting for her question.

"I'm spending next semester in Berlin and want Randy with me," I said.

"That'll take some doing," Erika agreed, and our confab began.

Chapter 50

"What did your parents say about you studying in Berlin?" Erika asked.

"They couldn't refuse me permission after saying that it would be OK for Melanie."

"She's going on a school trip?"

"Yes."

"For how long?"

"Two weeks," I replied.

"That's different," Erika said, and I nodded.

"OK, to summarize, you want to live in Berlin for at least three months, together with Randy, and he doesn't yet know. Nor do his parents who pay for his college and give him enough money to survive."

"That's about it," I said.

"You *do* have a problem."

"That's why I'm asking," I said.

Erika thought silently while I looked about the room. It had long been her refuge from continuing pain: the death of her mother and sister years before.

The room had been re-decorated since I had last been here. This had become a habit, her attempt to change what could not be changed, I once thought. When her father complained at the cost, she replied, "It's cheaper than if I used drugs," and he never protested again.

Margaret in Berlin

Before, the room had a cottage-in-the-country style with its pine bed and chests, wash-stands, lace mini-prints, and rug covered stripped floors. Now, the brass bed, dressing tables with muslin skirts, flower-printed walls and period fireplace with mantel placed it in the English Edwardian era.

Erika sat up straighter and sighed. I looked at her, hopefully.

"What do you think that Randy will say?" she asked.

"You know Randy: any change makes him nervous. He still faints at the sight of blood and must be dragged for a flu shot. Apart from his parents' objection, which I expect, studying in Germany would be a huge change. He'll refuse," I said.

"Unless you make it worth his while," Erika said.

"How would I do that?"

"What's the strongest material in the world?" Erika asked, with a smile.

"I don't know. Steel alloyed with cobalt? That's just a guess. What is it?" I asked, a bit angrily.

My problem was too serious for games. It had nothing to do with science. But Erika had already thought of a solution and was leading me toward it.

"No, take another guess," she teased, with the same knowing smile on her face.

"Erika," I said, warningly.

"I'm sorry. I'm furious about being sick. The strongest material is a woman's pubic hair. It can pull a man half-way around the globe," she said,

Now, she wasn't smiling.

Chapter 51

"That sounds like a good line but I don't get it," I confessed, feeling stupid.

"I stole it from Hillary," Erika said.

Hillary is my other best friend. She and Erika's personalities had grated each other until Hillary gave birth prematurely. Erika supported and suffered with her through this painful experience and both were changed by it. After that they became close.

"It *is* a good line," I repeated, though still not grasping its meaning.

"That's what I told Hillary. She said that it was Bill's," Erika added.

"Bill" or "my Billy" as Hillary affectionately speaks of him, is the ex-President of the United States, Bill Clinton. He lives in Chappaqua, New York, a few miles from Greenwich. Hillary became infatuated with his photo soon after discovering sex, which came early for her. Thereafter, she read his books and stalked him as closely as she could considering that he has both Secret Service and wife protection.

Hillary, *my* Hillary, has strongly implied though never actually stated that Bill is the lover who vanished from her life after she became pregnant with their child, Angelina.

Erika, my go-to resource for psychological puzzles, explained it like this: "Hillary has never had a real father so she chose the father of our country for a lover." Explaining Bill's behavior "is above my pay grade," Erika added.

It suddenly hit me what Erika was suggesting.

"You're saying that if I seduce Randy, he'll ignore his fears *and* his parents' objections and accompany me to Europe," I said.

"Don't put yourself down: you're lovelier than you imagine. Why do you think the bodyguards compliment you though if they went further Vladimir would have their head. And don't lie that you haven't thought of having sex. Or maybe you already have and I'm preaching to the converted."

"No, not yet. We've done everything but that. I have this thing about waiting until we're married," I confessed.

"Well, Clarence and I haven't waited though I won't claim that it's peaches and roses," Erika said.

I sprawled more comfortably on the chaise lounge, awaiting Erika's story. Today has been filled with surprises, I told myself.

Chapter 52

Erika snuggled in bed and looked up at the ceiling. After a minute of waiting, I asked, "What's the problem?"

"You must have seen the commercials," Erika said, in a condescending tone.

I had no idea what she referred to. Obviously, my brain had been weak that evening.

"ED, Erectile Dysfunction," Erika said.

Her tone was more tired than angry.

I said nothing. To question a person about their sex life is to enter a minefield and I had no intention of going there without a firm invitation.

"OK," I said slowly, and waited.

"His erection droops once he nears me. It's like it's scared to death," Erika said.

What do I say now? I asked myself. Though goodhearted, Erika *is* intimidating. She's very smart and forceful and doesn't tolerate fools, or failure.

Clarence has failures on his resume. Despite being a genius with computers and possessing the high intelligence that comes genetically from having two parents with doctorates, he never graduated from high school. His huge size made him a target of bullying and he chose to drop out before reacting violently. Thereafter, he was home-schooled.

He and his parents now work in their startup. It is funded by three hedge funds and could become the next Google.

Menstrual cramps I know about and even pregnancy from following those of friends. But Erectile Dysfunction was out of my league. Still, I felt that I should say something.

"Could Clarence's problem be related to his diabetes?" I asked.

"His doctor doesn't think so. He suggested therapy," Erika replied.

"And?"

"I raised the issue with my therapist. He's willing to treat us as a couple but Clarence isn't psychologically minded. He thinks that therapy is for weak people."

"But he knows that you're in therapy," I said, feeling puzzled.

"It makes no sense, does it? Therapy is for weak people but I'm strong and in therapy. His penis' drooping might be caused by his unconscious fear that my influence will weaken him, cut it off, so to speak."

"Is that your's or your therapist's interpretation?" I asked.

"His, but it does make sense," Erika replied.

"So what do you plan to do?" I asked.

"Damned if I know except to keep trying," Erika said, with an accepting tone.

That seems as good a solution as any, I thought, but didn't say.

Chapter 53

Years before, in preparation for *the* day, Erika had gotten a prescription for birth control pills from her considerate pediatrician. Being thorough, she also purchased condoms but I was puzzled why she had bought so many: five packages, each containing thirty-six Trojan Ultra-Thin Lubricated. Her explanation had nothing to do with sex.

"They were on sale," she said.

Despite her family's wealth, Erika is frugal. I did her nails throughout high school though her father could have bought her a nail salon or even two shops or a hundred.

By then, we regarded ourselves as sisters. "What's mine is yours," she would always insist.

"You still have your room here," Erika pressed.

I understood what she meant. Erika is as thoughtful as a friend can be and I knew she was serious.

After leaving Erika's room, I checked the nightstand in the bedroom that I usually occupy when staying overnight. An unopened thirty-six condom package still lay here. Its expiration date was three years hence. I had time to decide.

Deciding when to first have sex is not a simple matter for many people. Mormons have guidelines as do members of most religions. Some people follow them religiously, to make another of my small puns, while others do not.

My family is flexible. Were it not, I would not have been allowed to date Randy who isn't Mormon. Nor to begin couple rather than only group dating at thirteen though most wouldn't have described our activity then as constituting a "date."

Margaret in Berlin

Would my adoptive or biological parents care if I had sex before marrying? Not at all. Melody, my oldest sister, lost (surrendered?) her virginity at seventeen to a customer she met while waitressing. Like most of the people who hope to enter the entertainment industry, Melody is the ultra-friendly type.

But having sex would be a big decision for me and Randy. Should I raise this issue with him in my home or his? I asked myself. *Neither*, I replied, not with our mothers hovering in the background!

OK, I decided, we'll visit Erika tomorrow, to bring cookies to cheer her. There, we'll be next to *our* bedroom while her father will be at work.

Chapter 54

I could have slept-over at Erika's house but considered it best to return home. It was good that I did since my father was waiting for me.

"Nina called and your mother wants me to speak with you," my father said, in a stern tone.

This comes from living in a small town. It would never happen in New York City or Berlin, I thought. But I also felt a bit pleased since Nina's call meant that people cared.

"Because I was speeding?" I asked, already knowing.

"Precisely."

"I promise to drive more carefully. I don't want an accident either," I said.

"OK. We know that you've got a lot on your mind but want you to reach adulthood healthy too," my father said.

I nodded agreement.

"Do you have time for a talk?" I asked.

The question seemed to burst out since I hadn't meant to ask for my father's advice.

"Always."

"I want Randy to come with me to Berlin," I confessed.

"That sounds reasonable."

I had expected an argument but his reply came after the briefest hesitation. Surprise caused me to become momentarily speechless. I sat down and he joined me on the sofa.

"A three-month separation is a long time. While I trust Randy, neither of us has dated anyone else. There are many fascinating girls at Yale and, like they say, out of sight, out of mind, Skype contact regardless."

"Are you asking for my romantic advice?"

"I guess that I am," I replied.

"Do you remember Collen and Milly?" my father asked, after several moments of silence.

I nodded. They had been members of our church before they moved to Santa Fe.

"Well, they had marriage problem for years. Collen asked his wife for a divorce several times but she had always refused. One day, after meeting a beautiful model, he asked his wife again and this time she agreed.

"Though I don't handle divorce cases, we were friends and he came to me for advice. He was filled with joy until I made a chance remark.

"'Probably Milly has found someone too,' I said.

"I don't know why I said it but Collen immediately became nervous. He rushed off, stormed into his wife's workplace, past her desk and into the office of her unsuspecting boss who he had decided was her lover. When his wife finally had him out of the office and back in his car, he recognized that he had his wife back and that this was what he really wanted.

"A year later, when I asked if he was sorry about the decision that he made, he replied, 'No, it was probably for the best.'"

My father looked intently into my face.

"Those who think that they can maintain love without troubles usually lose their way," he said.

With that, my father rose, kissed me on the forehead, and went to bed.

Chapter 55

Soon after my father returned to work, our family's finances returned to its former prosperity. Among the first family purchases, at the pleading of all four children, were a home internet connection and Netflix. My youngest sister, Claudine, watched Disney shows, teenage Melanie caught up with the teenage dramas, and my older sister, Melody, watched foreign movies that few have heard of.

Melody, is a budding film critic. She *loves* movies and sees her life's task as being to raise artistic taste. When home, I'm often dragged into her room to watch her latest discovery and suffer its critical review.

Our parents know better than to ask what Melody views. Still, though disliking its content, my religious mother would have been pleased to learn of that night's movie for it would strengthen her conviction of an all-embracing Godly intelligence in the universe. It was the Norwegian film, *Turn Me On, Dammit!* and its title tells all.

The movie is about Alma, a teenager who has just discovered sex. She reminded me of my friend, Hillary, as she was years before. Alma lives in a small, exceptionally boring town miles from anywhere. She first tries to satisfy herself through phone sex, and then with a boy she loves who has a hard time talking. Just like Randy, I thought.

Though appealing, the movie is slow-moving and I soon tuned it out as my thoughts turned to my current problem: How to turn sexually fearful Randy into a stud.

"It's not hard to get sex. All you have to do is stay in a bar until 3AM and lower your standards," Melody had said suddenly.

Margaret in Berlin

"Huh?"

"Alma wants sex and doesn't know how to get it," Melody answered.

"She's under-age and maybe there's no bar in her tiny town," I replied.

My thinking returned to Randy. I would invite him to visit Erika with me. If he objected, I would treat him like I would if he was my husband. I would insist that she was a friend to both of us and that helping a friend is not a choice but a duty.

Then I would hug him and, if my body couldn't seduce him into the bedroom, I would offer him pot-laced brownies. Erika can get them. She can get anything. If Randy wasn't hungry, I would push him onto the floor and rape him. I've heard of such things happening.

Having these thoughts, I realized that, like fifteen-year-old Alma in the movie, I was losing it. Melody interrupted my delusions.

"Sex is simple. It's life that makes it complicated," she said.

You don't know the half of it, I thought.

Chapter 56

After leaving Melody's room, I decided *not* to drug Randy with pot brownies or try to rape him. The movie had gotten to me and I was four-years older than its character, Alma. Instead, I simply invited Randy to visit Erika and he accepted. The next morning, I drove to a Greenwich institution, the St. Moritz bakery on Greenwich Avenue.

The store is small, cute, and has been here since the beginning of time or that's how it seems. Commuters make it a required stop before catching the morning train to Manhattan though if you're looking for only coffee I'd go down the street to Starbucks.

The St. Moritz' products are phenomenal but expensive. This explains why our family hadn't shopped there in years. As usual, finding nearby parking was a problem but Greenwich is a small town and I love to walk.

As a child, I had loved the bakery's Owls, Pandas, and Pupcakes. These are cupcakes with the proper shapes and chocolate and vanilla frosting.

Erika and I are into healthy eating and tend to avoid sweets. Randy gorges on fast-food. My hassling him has had no effect. Things will be different once we're married, I vowed to myself—and hoped. Caring for a sickly young husband isn't the future that I'm seeking.

But this situation was special. Having read online that chocolate had aphrodisiac qualities, I bought Chocolate Covered Strawberries and Flourless Chocolate Cake for Randy. For Erika, I bought a French Apple Tart. It seemed the healthiest treat being sold that day.

Margaret in Berlin

With these purchases, and the thought of the thirty-six Trojan Ultra-Thin Lubricated condoms in the night-table, I went to war. A battle of the sexes for sex, I told myself. To paraphrase Melody: Though sex is simple, it can certainly drive a person crazy.

I picked up Randy at his house.

"What's that?" he asked, noting the boxes on the rear seat.

"Treats for my favorite people," I replied, as I backed out of the driveway.

After buckling his seat belt, Randy placed a possessive hand high up my thigh. Is this an omen? Has God answered my prayer? I asked myself.

Chapter 57

Fearing a speeding ticket, I deliberately drove five miles under the speed limit. But it was hard to keep my mind on the road with Randy rhythmically squeezing my thigh. At a stop sign, I took my eyes off the road, gazed dreamily at him, and spoke softly.

"Nice, but more slowly," I said, squeezing my thighs together and acting out a scene from some movie.

We must teach each other what we like sexually, I thought, as Randy obliged.

Randy held the cake boxes in front of his pants as we entered Erika's house. This is another good omen, I told myself.

Igor opened the door. He is the biggest flirt of all the bodyguards. He noted Randy's flushed face, the position of the packages, and smiled. He didn't ask any questions. I am considered a member of the household and Randy's was a familiar face.

I waved to the passing housekeeper and went to the kitchen for knives, forks, and dishes. Then we hurried up the stairs to Erika's room.

As we entered, Erika was sitting up in bed reading from her Kindle. She looked toward us expectantly, like the director of a play who awaits its opening performance.

The bed and condoms lay next door. That room had its own private bathroom, for Randy and me to shower together afterward, when the housekeeper would bring us whatever snacks we desired. For guests, Erika's house resembles a luxurious hotel.

"I brought these for dessert," I said, placing the box containing the French Apple Tart on the bed together with a plate, knife, and fork. Then I distanced myself from mono-infected Erika and sat on the chaise lounge with Randy.

"What's in the other box?" Erika asked, with a sly grin.

"A chocolate feast, Chocolate Covered Strawberries and a Flourless Chocolate Cake. *You* get the healthier treat," I replied.

"Gorging on chocolate," Erika said, archly, with a smile.

She obviously knew about chocolate's aphrodisiac reputation.

"Yes, all for my man," I said, in a husky voice.

Melody's movies are a big help, I thought.

I moved closer to Randy and rested my hand on his thigh. Act One had begun.

Chapter 58

Throughout the years when Erika and I managed our babysitting business, we had held a monthly group meeting for the babysitters. These discussions officially concerned child care issues but, as one would expect with teenagers, the talk frequently turned to dating problems and sex.

An early question, since most of us were still virgin, was whether a woman always bled the first time that she had sex. During that meeting a local gynecologist was present and she answered "not always but sometimes."

The doctor explained that bleeding occurs at the breaking of the hymen, a thin piece of skin which partially covers the entrance to the vagina. She said that the breakage of the hymen can go unnoticed and also occur through sports or tampon use.

I didn't know whether there would be bleeding when I first had sex since I had long used tampons and been involved in sports. There *was* bleeding that morning but, alas, it wasn't mine. Like they say, man proposes and God disposes, or maybe you believe in fate.

What happened was this. While enthusiastically talking and snacking, Erika absentmindedly moved the fork toward her mouth. Only at the last moment did she sense that the fork was aimed straight for her face. She quickly changed its direction but banged herself in the nose with the side of her hand.

Blood dripped from her nose onto the coverlet. At this sight, Randy bolted upright and fainted dead away. I caught him and lowered him to the ground as Erika pressed the alarm button beside her bed.

Moments later, a bodyguard rushed into the room with pistol drawn. Seeing blood and Randy on the floor, he barked Russian into his phone and was soon joined by another bodyguard. I knew her to have been a doctor in the Russian military. I calmly provided the explanation that I had been given years earlier.

"Randy faints at the sight of blood. It's a vasovagal attack and nothing to worry about. Emotional shock caused blood to rush from his brain to his stomach causing the faint. After laying flat, the blood returns to his brain. He'll be fine in a moment."

Randy supported my description by opening his eyes and speaking. The doctor examined him and pronounced him fine. She diagnosed Erika's nosebleed as being trivial. It resulted from the blow to her nose and the dryness of the room. She told Erika to pinch her nostrils shut for ten minutes and breathe through her mouth. While waiting, she asked Randy what he was studying.

"Pre-Med, to become a doctor," he replied, weakly.

The doctor stared and shook her head.

"His father is a doctor and insists that Randy become one too," I said.

The doctor continued staring.

When the bodyguards had left and Randy went to the bathroom, I turned toward Erika.

"That wasn't the bleeding that I hoped for," I said.

Erika just smiled.

Chapter 59

The atmosphere in Erika's bedroom seemed unusually quiet after the recent commotion. Erika leaned back in bed and I lay on the chaise lounge. It had been my favorite position for years. A change of topic seemed in order.

"How is Pamela?" I asked.

"I don't know since she's not talking much. After buying what she needed, she spoke with her father but that's about it. She's afraid to leave the house though I can't imagine her husband finding her here," Erika replied.

"He's a lawyer and lawyers have resources," I said.

Our talk died off, neither of us being in the mood. My plan to have sex with Randy had failed and Erika's nosebleed added to the feeling one gets that their disabling illness will never end—until the day that it does.

"Pamela will probably drop in. She usually does about this time," Erika said.

Almost as if on cue, Pamela walked through the open doorway.

She was dressed Western style in an open-necked shirt, jeans, and boots. Upon entering the room, she looked hungrily toward the chaise lounge that I occupied. It had apparently become her favored place too. She sat in a club chair and attempted a smile.

"The belt was Abram's suggestion. He said that she needs to be *packed*. Show it to Margaret," Erika said.

Pamela removed a narrow, V-shaped knife that was inconspicuously concealed within the buckle and handed it to me. It was razor-sharp and I held it gingerly. I looked toward her.

"Do you know how to use this?" I asked Pamela, but it was Erika who replied.

"Abram is teaching her self-defense. He's taking her to the Range tomorrow," she said, looking as happy as a mother who has just seen her baby take its first steps.

Erika referred to the Greenwich Pistol Range where she had learned to shoot. I nodded, and carefully returned the knife. After a month of training with Abram, I would have no concern for Pamela's safety. But I did have one question.

"Great Britain is uptight about guns. Is this knife legal there?" I asked.

"Probably not and I won't take it with me when I leave. But it gives me confidence for now," Pamela replied.

After the silence that followed, I spoke my sudden worrying thought.

"Randy has been gone for a while. What could have happened to him?" I asked, rhetorically, and left the room to look.

Chapter 60

I met the housekeeper in the hall.

"Have you seen Randy?" I asked her.

"I saw him go downstairs a few minutes ago," she replied.

Maybe Randy went to the kitchen for a drink, I thought, and hurried downstairs. After not finding Randy in the kitchen, I began worrying. He is shy and it's not like him to go off on his own when we are together. Upon leaving the kitchen, I met Abram.

"Have you seen Randy?" I asked.

"Yes, he left the house a few minutes ago."

My purse was upstairs but I already carried what I needed: cellphone, car keys, and driver's license in my wallet.

I phoned Randy but my call went to his voicemail. Maybe he has grown tired of girl-talk and decided to go home, I thought. His home was only four miles from Erika's house and easily walked. Despite his recent faint and many fears, Randy is physically healthy and Greenwich is a safe town, I reassured myself.

A half-mile down the road, I spotted Randy walking and stopped the car beside him. I rolled down the window.

"Get in," I said.

He ignored me and kept walking.

"Randy, please get in. You're worrying me," I pleaded.

His gait slowed and he finally stopped. Once seated in the car, he wouldn't look at me.

"Why did you run off like that?" I asked.

Concern had made my tone harsher than I intended.

Randy covered his face with his hands.

"I'm hopeless, a total failure. I should kill myself," he said.

A car isn't the place for this type of conversation. Nor is someplace with others around, I told myself.

"Randy, I love you and we need to talk but not here. We'll go where we used to sit. Buckle up," I said.

Though not replying and with downcast face, he buckled up after a few moments and I drove toward town.

Every couple has their own special place. It might be where they first met or spent their happiest hours. For us, it is the tiny park on Greenwich Avenue. Encased by greenery and enclosed by towering trees, it is a lover's oasis for teenagers having no place to go.

We had often spoken there during times of crisis. Memories of overcoming them lingered and I prayed that, once again, we would be so blessed.

Chapter 61

I managed to find a parking space one block from the park and we walked there slowly. Randy didn't take my hand as he usually did so I took his.

The park was nearly empty. So was the bench on which we had sat. It was a year since we were last there and much had happened in both of our lives since then. But I still felt guilty for this didn't excuse my failure to recognize how depressed Randy had been.

Long before, after the murder of her mother and sister, Erika determined to throw herself under an oncoming train at the Greenwich Station. Only the chance greeting by her father's friend had saved her, wrenching her free from the tunnel vision of depression that had enveloped her.

Was Randy's mind like that now? Has his despair gone this far? I asked myself. I feared that trying to help him was far outside my league but began anyway.

I strongly grasped both of his hands as I spoke. For emotional support and to make sure that he didn't run away.

"How long have you felt sad?" I asked.

Randy stared at our joined hands, as if they were hieroglyphics that he was trying to decipher.

"Maybe forever," he said finally, in a low tone.

"OK. Would you see Erika's therapist? She's seen him for years and says that he's great," I said softly.

"No!" he said, forcefully.

"OK, but do I have to be afraid that you'll hurt yourself?" I asked.

This was the crucial question. If his reply was 'yes,' I would have to inform his parents since he belonged in a hospital. My biological mother, Lena, owned and managed the psychiatric hospital in town. I could visit him every day.

"You don't have to worry. I just get like this. I'm fed up and dread my pre-med classes though I'm doing great in them."

"You always do well," I said, supportively.

"Except with people."

"Many would gladly change places with you," I said.

My remark produced his pale smile, and I relaxed.

"I'm going to Austin this weekend," Randy said.

"Why?" I asked.

"With my advisor, for a conference on computer modeling of the nervous system. I'm the class's coding expert."

"You need a change," I said, with a smile.

Then worrisome thoughts entered my mind: Randy is depressed; suicide is most often carried out with a gun; guns are as freely sold as Hershey bars in Texas; Randy shouldn't be alone. I didn't speak these ideas for it wouldn't have been helpful. But I would never forgive myself if I lost him.

"I'll come with you. We need each other," I said.

"You never forget those that you've lost. You just try to stop listening to their voices in your head," Vladimir had once told me.

Chapter 62

My parents accepted this news calmly. After learning of the dangers that I had experienced in London and Tokyo, Austin seemed as safe as a Greenwich pre-school.

I didn't have to ask them for money since I had earlier phoned Vladimir.

"Papa, you suggested that the company might open an American branch. Randy is going to a conference in Austin which is considered the next Silicon Valley. Keeping a startup's founder and their family safe would be a business priority. I thought of going with Randy to make sales contacts," I said.

"Good thinking. Take the corporate credit card from the safety deposit box. Invite managers and politicians to dinner and don't stint on expenses. I'll FedEx you our latest brochures," Vladimir said.

After our conversation ended, I was pleased with my cleverness. It's always best to have someone whose agreement you need believe that what you want to do is really their idea.

Then, for some unknown reason, something that my Greenwich lawyer-father had said came to mind: When you see a clear road to success, the chances are that there is something wrong.

But that day I was feeling too happy to accept this gloomy proverb. Randy and I will have our pre-marital honeymoon in Austin and everything will be alright, I had told myself–while praying that it would be true.

Chapter 63

I had told Randy that I would make all the travel arrangements and he was glad to let me. This was how our relationship had always been: Ying and Yang, I handled the bothersome practical details so he could get on with being a genius. I didn't see this as being feminist or anti-feminist. It is just how things work best with us. Things might be different with you and your lover.

Although Randy had possessively placed his hand up my thigh and earlier explored my body, we never had sex. Not even oral sex which many girls don't consider real sex and a way to retain their self-image as a virgin. Some girls even consider anal sex this way.

Randy is not good at communication. Did he believe that I would book two hotel rooms or one? Booking one room would tell him that Austin was to be our honeymoon. Randy isn't a social genius but he is a quick learner. Sex will be a learning experience for both of us, I concluded.

Wanting us to be relaxed, I decided that it would be best for us to have a good night's sleep before leaving and scheduled a non-stop flight leaving Newark Airport at 2:20PM. Our family had been poor for so long that springing for the Business Class made me nervous. But we are no longer poor and the trip is a business expense too, I reminded myself. The credit card, which I had picked up from the company's safety deposit box in Manhattan on the previous day, had a $250,000 limit. I didn't expect to exceed it.

Erika drove us to the airport and gave me a knowing look in the departure lounge. While smiling sweetly, I remembered what I had forgotten to pack: the box of thirty-six Trojan Ultra-Thin Lubricated condoms lay in the nightstand at Erika's home.

Well, this might be for the best, I reassured myself. Viewing their inspection by a TSA agent would shock nervous Randy. Better to take things one step at a time. I'll buy condoms in Austin.

This mental note I wrote down.

Chapter 64

My family didn't fly after my father became ill with Lyme disease. Not because any of us feared flying but because we couldn't afford it. My dad had closed his law practice and received Social Security Disability payments and Food Stamps. These and food from the Mormon Food Bank and produce from friendly local farmers kept us from starving.

The few flights that I had taken—to Tokyo after winning an essay prize, and to London, which my wealthy English grandmother had paid for—were less exasperating than this flight.

The security line moved slowly, which didn't appear to trouble the TSA agents. We made it through the long line to the checkpoint before you step through the imaging portal. The woman in front of us was similar to me. She was young, Caucasian, wore little jewelry, and was casually dressed.

For whatever reason she had been pulled out of the line and told that she had been "randomly selected for additional screening." When the woman asked why, she was ordered to stand off to a side and prepare for a pat down. I couldn't see anything suspicious about her. She looked like a college student.

As I took off my shoes and placed my small belongings in the bin, I watched and listened to what was going on with the woman.

The TSA agent spoke her monotone about what would happen: the areas she had to touch and how she was going to do it. The woman protested but was told that it was either to accept this or she would miss her flight. She asked if there was a private room that they could go to or a screen that she could step behind and was told that there wasn't.

The pat down went in the usual places: shoulders, neck, breasts, stomach, arms and legs. The agent stopped at the woman's knees and said that she was now going to inspect her inner thighs and groin areas. The woman was visibly upset but agreed and the pat down continued from her outer thighs to her inner thighs and crotch.

Something about the woman's crotch bothered the agent and she did it again. Then she said loudly that she had felt something "foreign and unusual" in the groin area. She called over another agent or supervisor and the woman was asked what was in her pants.

Obviously embarrassed, the woman said that she was on her period and wearing a menstrual pad. This wasn't good enough for the original agent who did another thorough feel of the woman's privates.

The agent asked, "Don't you wear tampons?" and the woman pleaded that she had run out of tampons. Having no time to buy more before leaving for the airport, she had borrowed a maxi pad from a relative.

I can't tell you what finally happened. Though taking as long as I could to put on my shoes and collect my belongings, I feared drawing attention and risking the same happening to me.

I was both pleased and alarmed by what Randy said as we exited security: "I'd kill anyone that did that to you."

Chapter 65

After leaving security, I looked for a place to hang out until departure. By now, Newark Airport was familiar to me and I introduced Randy to the Flora Café where I had been before. Randy isn't into healthy eating but he agreed to try both hummus and a veggie burger. Though admitting that he liked both, I may not succeed in turning him into a fellow vegetarian. Still, call me tiger mom or not, I intend for our children to grow up vegetarian.

This flight was less comfortable than my recent overseas one. Possibly because the planes were different, a Boeing 737 and not a Boeing 757, if that mattered. Here, the legroom was just bearable instead of the previous luxurious flat-bed seat that could recline into a bed. The food was little more than snacks too.

Still, the short flight, just under four hours, and having Randy to snuggle against, made the discomfort negligible.

Austin-Bergstrom International Airport is delightful. It's clean, well-run, has inviting décor, and live music. I had reserved a suite at the InterContinental Hotel. Knowing nothing about Austin, I chose it based on online reviews where it earned four out of five stars.

The hotel is a fifteen-story landmark within walking distance of the State Capital and the University of Texas at Austin. The room came with the usual: cable TV and Wi-Fi, a work desk, and a minibar which I hoped that Randy wouldn't use. The hotel also had an indoor pool, a spa, a gym, and a 24/7 business center. I planned to keep Randy too busy exploring my body to use any of these.

I would ordinarily have taken a simple room but, considering my promise to Vladimir to seek customers, having a suite made it suitable for meetings. The separate living room had a pull-out sofa which I didn't expect to get used. Still, if Randy met a researcher who was unable to find a room, it could be handy.

The hotel staff was professional and check-in went smoothly. I had made the reservation with the corporate credit card, and Randy didn't comment on my having reserved only one room.

I turned toward him.

"I forgot to bring some girl things. I'm going to get them at the drugstore," I said.

"Girl things" are a mystery to boys about which they never ask.

The bellhop took our bags and Randy followed him upstairs. As they left, I tried to remember the condom brand that Erika had purchased. Her buying skill is legendary.

Chapter 66

I asked the desk clerk for the location of the nearest pharmacy. Luckily, it was just one block away.

I felt uncomfortable buying condoms though they are no more personal an item than tampons. Feeling too embarrassed to ask a clerk for their location, I wandered the aisles until finding them.

The condoms lay on racks, stacked in packets of different colors. That they came in different sizes and even flavors caused me to wonder. I stood stunned, unable to remember what Erika had bought. What would Randy feel if the size were too large. The choice of condom wasn't something that our conversations had ever covered. It's a man's affair, right?

I stared for so long that a clerk sidled beside me. He might have considered me a fetishist.

"Can I help?" he asked.

His knowing smile aroused the memory that I had been seeking, and I took three packages of Trojan Ultra-Lubricated off the shelf. His smile broadened.

"No, I was just trying to remember what brand my husband buys," I said, affecting a wifely tone.

As the clerk moved away, I considered asking Randy to buy tampons for me before leaving Austin.

I walked slowly back to the hotel, trying out various lines in my head. Some might cause him to regard *me* as seducing *him*. How would this make him feel? But what is the difference since the end result is the same? I asked myself.

Still, boys don't like for girls to take charge and particularly with regard to sex. But sex concerns bodies and not cute phrases, I reassured myself, as I entered our room. For me, this was a sound deduction.

Randy was reading the conference schedule though the luggage lay unpacked. He relied on his mother to do such things for him and I had slowly adopted this role. When we began dating, he would ignore his mother's demand that he gets a haircut but not mine though I'm not a stickler for such things.

"Did you get what you needed?" Randy asked.

"What we needed," I said, softly.

"Huh?" Randy said, not having looked up or grasped my meaning.

I gave up and began unpacking.

"I've been invited to attend a forum at eight-thirty so we should eat now," Randy said, again without looking up.

"OK, will you return very late?" I asked.

"I'm not sure. They've sometimes been all-nighters," he replied.

Chapter 67

My annoyance at Randy's casual comment, that his meeting might be an "all-nighter," caused me to do what a lover should never do: pick an argument.

"What could be *so* important that you'd stay out all night?" I asked.

I omitted the rest of my thought, "and off my body."

Randy gave me a withering, pitying stare.

"Do you know *anything* about artificial intelligence? How important it will be in the future?"

"Yes," I said, softly, already regretting my outburst.

Randy's tone lowered too. Neither one of us really wanted to fight.

"Computers can beat us at some things easily. Like playing chess or a board game so long as we've programmed them first. But things that people find simple are incredibly difficult for machines: driving a car or spotting an object in a photo.

"To do these things, computers must be taught *deep learning* which is modeled on the human brain. This enables them to ignore all but the most important characteristics of a sound or image. It will open the door to self-driving cars, and medical programs which can do many jobs better than doctors."

"But won't that radically change lives? Put people with jobs like truck driving out of work?" I asked.

I hoped that my question would have Randy feel that I was back by his side. He didn't ordinarily blow up no matter what I said. I feared that his depression had regained its hold. Or is it something that I haven't recognized? I asked myself.

"It will, and that's why this conference is important. It's not concerned with something like making a better search engine though that probably will be discussed. It's about changing society, *really* pulling us into the computer age.

"And you're right about truck drivers. They could disappear since driverless vehicles will cover the same routes more quickly and safely. What company would rather choose error-prone human drivers? They'll lose their jobs in the coming age of intelligent machines."

"I can see why you might be up all night," I said, with a suitably repentant tone.

Randy nodded and smiled.

"I get too heated sometimes. Let's go eat, love," he said, apologetically.

Chapter 68

I would usually have first checked the restaurant reviews online but Randy's recent behavior had scattered my mind. His talk of suicide in Greenwich and angry flare-up was unlike him. So, having noticed that a restaurant adjoined the hotel, I suggested that we go there and he readily agreed. The convention center, where his meetings were being held, was only a ten-minute walk from the hotel. I wanted him close by me even if not with me.

Eating out is a chore for vegetarians though I'm not a rigid foodie. I eat fish and don't give meat-eating companions nasty stares. Each to their own is my motto. Having heard that Texas eateries are prized for their barbecue, I feared that my dinner would wind up being salad but was pleasantly surprised.

"The Roaring Fork is an Austin institution. It's known for its wood-fired steaks," the hotel concierge had said. I simply smiled and said that we'd give it a try.

Meat might be the preference of most Texans but the Roaring Fork offered far more. While being seated, I vowed to myself that I wouldn't criticize whatever Randy ordered. Even if it were steak smothered in bacon fat!

Randy seemed on edge and that I hadn't figured out why upset me. I had always been able to sense Randy's moods and understand them but there now seemed a wall between us. Had something happened that he hadn't shared with me? I suddenly felt uneasy about our relationship. Was he involved with another girl? I asked myself.

We sat at the bar while waiting for a table. The blaring TV news wrenched personal worries from my mind. There had been another terrorist mass murder in America. The announcer added that such shootings were now the "new normal" and Austin was a high value target of opportunity. Local police were offering training to businesses on how to prepare for and react to an active shooter.

"It's worrying. Killing the famous people at the conference would make a big splash," Randy said, looking away from the TV.

"It could have happened here," I said.

"You can't live forever," Randy replied casually.

Considering his recent thought of suicide, I didn't find this comment reassuring. Nor did his following statement comfort me: "Maybe I should buy a gun while we're here."

Chapter 69

I tried to stop worrying by concentrating on the food, which was wonderful. For appetizer, I had guacamole with tortilla chips: very Tex-Mex and vegetarian too. Randy chose tortillas with Green Chili Pork. I said nothing.

Following this, we both had the Mixed Market Greens but a different "Specialty of the House." Mine was Blackened Redfish and his was The Roaring Fork "Big Ass" Burger which is basically a hamburger with cheese and bacon. Again, I didn't say anything but couldn't help hoping that his breath didn't stink of meat that night.

Our conversation was tedious, even forced. Not feeling that it was the right time to raise my concern about him, I spoke of his meeting that evening.

"Don't you find it boring, listening to people read their papers?" I asked.

I hated when being placed in that position and had always wondered why people tolerate it. They could stay home and read the later, printed papers in comfort.

"I don't like it either but this conference is different. Here, the paper's writer is given five minutes to describe it. Then, two experts are given five minutes each to critique the paper after which the floor is open for questions with everyone being friendly. Even toward people who are trying to show how smart they are but say dumb things."

"You won't have to prove anything. They'll *know* how smart you are," I said softly, doing everything but bat my eyes.

Randy put down his fork and took my hand.

"I'm sorry about how things have been lately. I've been going through a lot and haven't been myself. There are just so many decisions that I have to make," he said.

"It's alright. I love you and will always be here for you," I said.

I stared into his eyes and squeezed his hand. Randy smiled and briefly squeezed my hand in return. Then he picked up his fork and finished eating his salad.

This is all wrong, I told myself. Randy should have replied, "I love you too," or something like that. Not give me a smile and hand squeeze.

It was at that moment, just as the waiter arrived with his Huckleberry Cheesecake and my Flourless Chocolate Torte, that I became convinced that our relationship was in trouble. It seemed that, for him, our past intimacy had vanished and we danced on the brink of an unknown future.

Chapter 70

When we finished eating, Randy left me with a smile and a peck on the cheek. Like an uncaring parent gives to a not too bright child, I thought.

I considered going to the bar and making myself available but I'm not that kind of girl. Plus, my ability to pick up a man wasn't what I needed to prove.

For some unknown reason I felt like a wife who, after discovering that her husband has cheated, wonders why she hadn't picked up clues earlier. I rode the elevator to our room feeling clueless.

There, I sat up in bed and skimmed through several magazines that the last occupant had left. It had probably seemed sinful to the maid to trash them, like throwing out books.

They were likely left by a family since one magazine was for women and the other was for girls. Being grownup, I chose the woman's magazine. But the articles depressed me with their descriptions of how to get a better skin, and curls too if that was what your lover preferred.

The teenage magazine was more to the point: what should a girl do when her boyfriend says that he wants her back after she's seen him loving another girl? Slug him, I impulsively thought, before catching myself.

But why am I so worried since Randy is exceptionally shy? Going to parties terrifies him. The idea of him picking up a girl is ludicrous. Or is it and how well do I really know him? I asked myself, remembering what Erika had once said, "There are many fascinating girls at Yale." Did an aggressive student seduce him?

Margaret in Berlin

I left the bed and went to his suitcase which his mother had packed. She does such things for him and he would expect me to unpack, I told myself, losing any sense of guilt at prying.

The suitcase contained the usual: socks; underwear; jeans; and a suit and tie, all neatly folded. There was also dress shoes for a formal occasion. A small leather case held shaving gear, a comb, and antiperspirant. Nothing suspicious here.

I slipped my hand within the elasticized pocket of the suitcase. It held a belt suitable for wearing with the suit, and an unsealed manila envelope. I opened the envelope and dropped the contents onto the bed: a twelve-pack container of Trojan BareSkin condoms. Upon opening it, I found that four were missing.

Chapter 71

I sat on the bed, *twice* counting the condoms though there could be no doubt that four were missing. Had Randy been faithful and used the missing condoms to practice putting them on? I doubted that!

The conclusion was obvious: I had been faithful and he had not. Still, we had never vowed to be true to each other. It had just been a given, or at least my given.

I put the condoms back in their package and replaced it in the manila envelope which I returned to its hiding place. Had Randy hidden it poorly because he unconsciously *wanted me* to find them, to tell me something that he couldn't bear to speak? I didn't know but will find out that night, I promised myself.

A few minutes later, when my depression had lifted a bit, I felt that I couldn't bear to be alone any longer. So I went downstairs to the hotel bar, intending to read on my Kindle to avoid the come-ons that a single woman in a bar inevitably attracts.

It was early and the bar was only half-full. I sat at its empty end, ordered a club soda and lemon twist, and opened the Kindle. Without intending to, I became engrossed in the book, *Dead Wake*. It tells of the submarine sinking of the Lusitania during World War I. Many prominent Americans were killed and the author vividly describes their lives and fates.

I had reached the part of the book where the ship was torpedoed when a man approached. His string tie was askew and his eyes were glazed. He was obviously drunk and tried to pick me up.

"Hello, pretty woman?" he said, standing so closely that I smelled the alcohol on his breath.

I turned toward him.

"Thanks, but I'd rather be alone tonight," I said politely, and turned back to my book.

But some people won't take a hint and he was one of them. He seated himself on the bar stool beside me and placed his hand on my shoulder.

"Yawl from the East. I like Eastern women. I'll give you two-hundred bucks to sit on my face," he said.

His words had been loud enough for others to hear. The murmuring in the room quieted and people stared at us.

Suddenly, the anger that I felt toward Randy boiled over and focused on this drunk. I closed my Kindle, got up from my bar stool and stood back. Then, after giving him a broad, inviting smile, I slapped his face hard and kicked the bar stool from under him. He fell in a heap and all talk in the room ceased as I grabbed the empty water bottle on the bar.

"I'd kill you if you weren't obviously drunk," I said coldly, and more loudly than I intended.

While standing above him, I heard footsteps and whirled around, holding the bottle upraised. I was willing to take on all comers that night.

Chapter 72

The man approaching me raised his hands in a non-threatening gesture. The woman beside him strengthened this appearance.

"Whoa, young lady. I'm the hotel's manager and want to apologize," he said, and nodded toward the rear of the room.

Security men came quickly and hustled the drunk away. The rage still hadn't left me but the manager smiled and his voice was soft and calm. He was in his forties with dark brown hair that grayed about the temples. His eyes were wise and stamped deeply with pain and the cynicism that no smile could hide.

The woman's green eyes also smiled. Her skin was good and her cheekbones were prominent but not bony. Her dark brown hair was long and her lips were very red from lipstick that had been generously applied. She was about thirty-five and all woman.

"Hello," she said, in a pleasantly husky voice.

The manager reached out and I handed him the bottle. My rage instantly disappeared as I recalled the incident in London where I had nearly killed a man who tried to mug me.

"I shouldn't have reacted like that. I've had a rough day, and months too," I said, apologetically.

"No apology is needed. No man should treat a woman like that. It's good that you're not carrying a gun. You aren't, are you?" the woman asked.

"No, not now," I said.

I instantly realized that stress had lowered my self-control and caused me to tell more to these strangers than I should. I caught the quick glance between them. Are they thinking that I'm crazy?

"My father is in the security business. He's training me to manage it someday," I said, by way of explanation.

"Which one?" the man asked.

I fished a business card from my wallet and handed it to him. It was a handsome card, sturdy with impressive raised lettering. On its front was only the name of the company, Vladimir's name and corporate title and a European phone number. On the back of the card were the names of its three principals and their former positions: Russian general; retired British SIS (Secret Intelligence Service) officer; and retired official of the Central Intelligence Agency.

The man read both sides of the card slowly. Then he passed it to his companion who did the same.

"Sit with us. We might do business," he said.

I nodded soberly but grinned inside.

Vladimir will be proud of me, I thought.

Chapter 73

I tend to be emotionally cooler than others, wanting to bring things under intellectual control. And, like former alcoholics who always fear that they will relapse, my recurring nightmare is that one day I will behave impulsively and destroy the order that I had been trying to place on my life. Adoptive kids can be like that.

So my recent loss of self-control had shaken me. I might have killed the drunk with the bottle if the hotel manager hadn't intruded. And, Southern chivalry aside, killing someone in Texas will gain you jail time at the very least.

I had done what I hated: behaved impulsively and become a nearly screaming hysteric until the manager's presence stopped me. So maybe it is true that God watches over the deserving, I thought.

We had moved from the bar to a booth at the rear of the restaurant. I had recovered my composure and felt at ease.

"You can use a drink? What would you like?" the manager asked.

"Just water. I'm Mormon and don't drink alcohol," I said.

I had proclaimed this so often that I joked I should have it tattooed on my arm.

He waved over a waiter and ordered three bottles of water.

"I'm Harry. Marguerite doesn't drink either," he said, turning to his companion who turned toward me.

"Tell us about yourself," she said.

"There's not much to tell, I live in Greenwich, Connecticut and am in my second year at Barnard. I'm here for a computer conference with my boyfriend who attends Yale," I said.

"And your father owns a security company?" Harry asked.

"Yes."

"Are your parents divorced? How can he run a European business from America?" Harry asked.

"Vladimir is my biological father. My adoptive parents, with whom I've lived since birth, live in Greenwich. He's a lawyer," I replied.

"Marguerite is a lawyer too."

"I'm a prosecutor. It's good that you didn't wind up in court," Marguerite added.

"He was simply drunk and I should have walked away," I said, apologetically.

"Well, you taught him a lesson," Harry said, with a smile.

"Thank you, but I'm ashamed of how I behaved," I said, returning his smile.

"I saw you enter the bar. You looked upset."

"I was."

"Do you want to talk about it?" he asked, in a sympathetic tone.

Margaret in Berlin

A person shouldn't always trust their immediate instincts about people but I did with Harry. I sensed a fine core beneath his tough shell. That he tended to be deceptive, neglecting outward forms of grace because he lived amongst fakes and wanted to keep from them his secret: that he was both idealistic and gallant.

"Yes, I do want to talk about it. I need advice," I said.

Chapter 74

I wasn't sure when my craziness began. Was it when I discovered the missing condoms or had my stress been building: from worry that Vladimir was dying; and fear, a month earlier, that my friend, Kimberly, would die in prison.

Or it might have come from the built-up of stress over many years: overcoming what had been considered a deadly genetic illness; nearly being murdered in Tokyo and London; and living a childhood ground down by poverty. The mind can tolerate only so much until it begins breaking down.

I didn't tell Harry and Marguerite all this. That would have taken far too long and invited uncomfortable questions. But I did reveal enough so that they would understand me, and I felt liberated.

"I've gone through a lot. As a child I was diagnosed with a deadly genetic illness and the cure was only found later. Then my adoptive father caught Lyme disease and couldn't work which pushed our family into poverty. He recently recovered and began working again.

"After that my best friend was falsely arrested. You must have heard about it. She was *the Barnard killer*. Then Vladimir had a minor heart attack and, an hour ago, I learned that my fiancée has probably cheated on me. I know that others have had it worse but..."

It was while speaking with them that I first realized how much pain I had experienced. No wonder you're cracking up, I told myself.

I didn't have to describe what happened in London or Tokyo. They already looked shocked. When they recovered, Marguerite zeroed in on what worried me most, "How long have you two been dating? What makes you think that he's cheating?"

"Six and four. We've been dating six years and four condoms were missing from a package of twelve. I had believed that we *both* hadn't had sex. I intended for this weekend to be our pre-wedding honeymoon, to motivate Randy to attend college with me next semester in Berlin," I replied.

Chapter 75

"What do you plan to do?" Harry asked.

"Confront Randy and ask him what's going on?" I replied.

"Will he tell you the truth?" Harry asked.

"I expect so. He's a lousy liar," I replied.

"What will you do if he has another girl-friend?" Marguerite asked.

"That's my problem. I don't know," I said.

"Another problem is that you'll have to re-evaluate your image of yourself. If you could have made such a blunder about Randy after six years of knowing him, can you trust your conclusion about anything? It might be *this* that upsets you most though betrayal is a terrible sin," Harry said.

I thought for a moment before deciding that he was probably correct.

"You're a wise man," I told him.

"He's my Nestor," Marguerite said, affectionately, touching his arm.

"Huh?" I asked, not knowing the word.

"You should be ashamed not knowing, and a fellow Barnard student too," Marguerite said, in a kindly-toned one-up-man-ship.

"Nestor was one of the Argonauts, a band of heroes in Greek mythology who battled a monster, the Caledonian Boar. Homer portrayed him as being old and wise, one who was experienced enough to combine practical guidance with reflection. A person hardened by adventure and battle but mellowed by sorrow too.

"Nestor was full of good advice and stories. He was witty, sensitive, and humorous, being so persuasive that he left people who consulted him with the feeling that *they* had formulated the advice that he had given them. He was also a severe taskmaster, yet one who could persuade gracefully."

Then followed a period of silence. I looked about the restaurant, which was getting busy. When Harry finally spoke it was softly, in the voice of a cleric or the best of friends.

"Several years ago, a troubled employee asked me for advice. She had been married fourteen years. Her husband had recently inherited a great deal of money and changed. Whereas before, his life had revolved about she and their children, he now developed other interests: buying an expensive car, skiing with strangers she didn't know, and the suggestion of using drugs and being unfaithful. He began spending money irresponsibly and hangers-on appeared in every corner.

"Her sister advised her to immediately divorce, to get some of the remaining money for herself and the children before it was all gone. Her mother told her the same, that she was young and beautiful and could easily find another husband. But she wasn't sure what to do."

Harry stopped talking and sipped his water.

"What did you tell her?" Marguerite asked.

"I told her that when she married it was for better or worse. That while things had been better, if her husband came down with cancer she wouldn't be thinking of divorce. I told her that his behavior was a disease of sorts and that I thought she should remain with him, to stay and show that she cared.

"Some people believe they married the wrong person but it isn't so much that they were the wrong person but that they weren't the right one themselves that caused the break. A commitment isn't a commitment if we stop caring when certainty leaves."

In the silence that followed I digested what Harry had said.

"Thank you,' I said softly, having made my decision.

I rose to leave but Marguerite, after glancing at Harry and gaining his unspoken agreement, placed her hand on my arm and stopped me. Her eyes were tearful.

"We need your father's help," she said.

Chapter 76

"Our son has been kidnapped," Marguerite said.

She spoke this fact calmly, as if she had lived with this horror for some time and had finally accepted it. I moved toward her and nodded, to indicate that I was listening closely.

"My grandmother is Mexican. Our son, Rafael, was visiting her in Mexico City when it happened," Marguerite said.

I nodded again.

"Have you informed the FBI? I asked.

"No. The kidnappers warned us against that. And if we did, the FBI would contact the Mexican police which is riddled with corruption."

"How much money do they want?" I asked.

"It's not money they want. We would give them everything we have. But they want something from me that I can't give."

"What's that?"

Harry answered this question.

"Marguerite isn't simply a prosecutor. She's the Texas Attorney General. The kidnappers want a man who is a convicted drug king-pin and murderer released from Death Row."

"Huh! You do need help," I exclaimed, feeling momentarily speechless.

"Does your father's company take on this type of problem?" Marguerite asked, pleadingly.

I had the sense that Harry and Marguerite had exhausted all the options that they could think of. This was the moment for honesty.

"Vladimir and his associates have helped many people. I know little of their cases and what details I do know I can't reveal. But a few years ago they rescued a child from his kidnappers and returned him unharmed to his mother. This happened in Tokyo and I was involved. Their services are international."

"We'll pay whatever it costs," Harry said.

"Vladimir makes pricing decisions but I've never known him to turn anyone away. Recently, without charge, he helped the daughter of a British Civil Servant to flee her murderous husband and arranged for her protection. I'll call him from my room. Berlin time is nine hours ahead of Texas time so it'll be early morning there. He's usually up at five," I said.

I gathered their phone numbers, hugged Marguerite, shook hands with Harry, and left. The problem with Randy had left my mind.

Chapter 77

It was too early to phone Vladimir without waking him so, after going to my room, I lay on the sofa and brooded. I had intended to save the bed for our pre-marital honeymoon and had wanted it left unused. Randy might be sleeping in it alone tonight.

I tried out several approaches with him in my mind but none seemed best. I would have to play it by ear, I decided. Then I set the alarm clock to awaken me in two hours and took a nap.

Over the previous few days my dreams had involved having sex with Randy but this one was a nightmare. I walked along a corridor with two closed doors. Within one room lay the person who I was seeking but in the other room awaited the Angel of Death. I was entering one of the rooms when the alarm woke me.

I stretched, and phoned Vladimir. He used the affectionate Russian greeting that he usually did with me.

"Well, little daughter. What have you been up to?" he asked.

"I'm in Austin, and a couple that I met need your help. Her son has been kidnapped," I said, quickly.

"Why don't they call the FBI?" Vladimir asked, just as I had earlier asked them.

"Because the kidnapping occurred in Mexico and the FBI would inform the local authorities who are notoriously corrupt. Also, because the ransom demand could never be met."

"How much is it?"

"It's not money. The boy's mother is the Texas Attorney General and the kidnappers want their boss, who is a convicted killer, released from the state's Death Row."

"Do the parents have financial means?"

"Not like the company's usual wealthy clients. He manages the hotel that I'm staying at and she has a state salary. But as Texas' Attorney General, she's an important political figure."

Vladimir thought silently for several moments.

"Have the couple contact me. Tell them that, if they desire, our company would be pleased to attempt their son's rescue, as a humanitarian service without charge."

"Thank you," I said, softly.

"You like them?" Vladimir asked, perceptively.

"Very much so. They deserve a good deed."

"Well, the effect of some good deeds confer a blessing while the result of others can return to haunt you. Let's hope that our activities for them is the former," Vladimir said, before hanging up.

Chapter 78

Vladimir phoned me ten minutes later.

"I can't have anyone there for two days and with a kidnapping it's important to begin quickly. Speak to the parents and find out what happened. Pavel is retired in Austin. Call on him for whatever you need. He's old but still sharp and has contacts. Phone me daily and keep in mind that drug gangs aren't known for their decency."

"Yes, papa, I'll be careful," I said, in a dutiful tone.

I immediately called Harry who said that we could meet in his office. Marguerite was with him. Her eyes were red from crying.

"Vladimir agreed to help and said that there would be no fee. The company will provide its services as a humanitarian gesture. But it'll be two days before the team arrives and he wants me to gather information so they'll be able to begin work immediately," I said.

"Thank you," Marguerite said.

Harry placed an arm around her shoulder as she exhaled deeply.

"Now, when did the kidnapping happen, exactly what was in the ransom demand, and how was it delivered?" I asked.

My problem with Randy remained absent from my mind. Faithfulness was a trivial matter compared with this.

Marguerite looked off into distance, thinking deeply and organizing her thoughts like the lawyer she was. When she spoke, her words were like the bulleted paragraphs of a well-considered memo.

"Their demand was sent by E-mail," she said.

She opened her phone and handed it to me. The note read: "Rafael is charming and well, playing video games and snacking on the healthy food that we have provided him. We have a nurse caring for him and he believes that he is staying with an uncle.

"Whether this situation continues depends on you. Just as you love your son, we love our brother who faces execution. If he dies, your son will die and we will both mourn but these sorry events need not be.

"Our brother, Candido Rath, is a simple businessman and not a bad person. None of those who were killed were American and all were in our business where risk is expected.

"We hope to return your son to you: happy, healthy, and with memories of a pleasant few days. We will also pay you five million dollars, to compensate you for your pain and trouble. If more money is needed, to gain the cooperation of others, you need only ask and this will be provided. We are reasonable business people.

"Time is short. You will be contacted with further instructions."

"When is the execution scheduled?" I asked, handing back the phone.

"Rath dies in seventeen days," Harry said, somberly.

Chapter 79

I was out of my element and knew it. All of my knowledge about kidnapping came from novels written by authors of uncertain background. But I did my best. Until Vladimir's team arrived, Marguerite and Harry had no one but me. I turned toward her.

"You were certainly targeted but why would they believe that you could get someone off Death Row. If you were the prison's warden you might aid an escape but not in your position. Unless…"

"Unless what?" Harry asked.

"Unless they want your entrée into the prison system. No one would refuse the state's Attorney General anything," I said.

Both Harry and Marguerite nodded and I felt on a roll.

"Where do you live? Who is in your household? Who knew of your son's visit to his grandmother? How did the kidnapping happen?" I asked.

The questions burst from me. These seemed the basic facts that Vladimir's team would need when they arrived.

"We live on Northern Dancer Drive, overlooking the Westlake Hills. Since we both work long hours, Rafael is cared for by an au pair from Norway. She's been with us for two years and loves him. I'm sure that she isn't involved.

"Before that, we had another au pair for three years. I was a stay-at-home mom during Rafael's first year, before I was elected Attorney General," Marguerite said.

She became tearful so I threw a soft question to calm her.

"Vladimir's team may want someone to stay at your house. How large is it?" I asked.

"It's more house than we need, five-thousand square feet with six bedrooms and four-and-one-half baths. We'd have room to put them up. We chose it because it's close to several highly ranked elementary schools. Marguerite loved the kitchen and I appreciated that we didn't have adjoining neighbors," Harry said.

"Did you discuss Rafael's trip with anyone?" I asked.

"That's what we've been asking ourselves. I may have mentioned it at work but Harry doesn't share his personal life with his employees. But during the election campaign, my family details became public," Marguerite said.

I nodded and tried to think of another question.

Chapter 80

"Tell me about the kidnapping," I said.

I tried to make my tone sympathetic and hoped that I wasn't sounding like I was asking about a vacation that they had just taken.

"We were at home. The news of his kidnapping came in a phone call," Marguerite began, after wiping her eyes and blowing her nose.

"His grandmother phoned us. Rafael had been playing outside and then he suddenly wasn't. While she and the maid looked frantically for him, they received a phone call. The man said that Rafael was in good health and would remain so if his mother was *cooperative*. That was the word he used.

"He emphasized that Rafael's only memory of this experience would be of a pleasant holiday during which he played video games and watched cartoons. That the police must not be called and everyone's life should carry on as usual. Then I told Harry."

I looked toward him.

"I hooked up the house phone to a recording device and we waited. The call came an hour later," Harry said.

My next question was delicate. Before a ransom is paid, *proof of life* is demanded. This is needed since it's far safer for a kidnapper to murder the victim than to allow them to live and provide evidence. How could I ask this tactfully without using this distressing phrase?

"Did you speak to Rafael?" I asked.

"Yes. He said that he was with his uncle, Pablo. Having fun playing video games and playing with Pablo's dog which was a German Shepherd. He said that he liked staying with Pablo better than staying with his grandmother."

I exhaled deeply. Rafael was alive.

"Did you speak with Rafael since that first phone call?" I asked.

"Yes, they said that they would have him phone me each evening, to reassure me that he was OK. As he would remain so long as their brother lived. They said that if I asked him about his location the phone calls would end."

Marguerite remembered something else a moment later.

"They also asked if Rafael was taking any medication and I said that he wasn't," she said.

Harry stood abruptly with an angry look on his face.

"We can't sit around doing nothing!" he insisted.

"That's not what's happening," I said calmly. "When the team arrives, they'll need all the facts. One that seems unrelated now may prove crucial," I said.

"That makes sense," Harry said, sitting down after regaining his cool.

I nodded but didn't say what I was thinking. It *should* make sense. As a child, I had read it in a Sherlock Holmes story.

Chapter 81

Marguerite and Harry rose from the sofa to return home and await the abductor's next call. But another question suddenly occurred to me.

"Drug dealers aren't known for their generosity. Why would the kidnappers pay you five million dollars when it's always the other way around?" I asked.

Both sat down again.

"Unless it's to trap you. Who would believe that a kidnapping had occurred or in an employee's innocence if, after an escape from a maximum security prison, it was learned that a worker had received a five-million-dollar payment?" I asked rhetorically, and then answered my question, *"No one."*

"I could refuse the money," Marguerite said.

"I doubt that you could. These people have already shown their sophistication. Identifying your bank account and wiring in the money would be simple for their money manager."

"So Rafael returns home and I go to jail," Marguerite said, after several moments of silence.

"That isn't what it sounds like to me. They'd rather have your help in the future too. But you aren't dealing with this alone. The team will soon be here and they're great people. Solving problems like this is their job,' I said, supportively.

"We'll pray for that, and for Rafael," Harry said, with a sigh.

Then, a moment later, "What are you doing tonight?" he asked me.

'Nothing really. Just go back to my room and think about my boyfriend. Randy won't be home for a few hours and maybe not tonight if there's an all-nighter. It's not unusual for hackers and he's a star," I said.

'You shouldn't be alone. Come home with us. Harry can drive you back to the hotel while I wait at the phone," Marguerite said.

"That's kind of you but you probably want to be alone," I said.

"No one should brood alone with problems, neither you nor us," Harry said.

Harry's car was a Prius, one of the environmentally friendly hybrids which are popular in tech-oriented Austin. He drove fast but carefully, being anxious to get home.

There, my usual dilemma arose when eating with strangers: being a vegetarian in a land of meat-lovers.

"What food do you like?" Marguerite asked, as we entered the house.

"I'm a vegetarian but also flexible so whatever you have," I replied.

"That's a coincidence. So are we," Marguerite replied, with her first real smile of the evening.

Chapter 82

Our dinner that evening would be applauded by vegetarians: Boca burgers, salad, and soy-based cheese, with blueberry pie for dessert

"Harry does the cooking when he's home. I could never get into it," Marguerite said, and I felt like hugging her.

Being a lousy cook had always made me feel inadequate. As if I lacked the cooking gene which all girls are supposedly born with. My only cookery accomplishment was an edible toasted cheese sandwich. I had finally met another woman like me.

After dinner we sat in the living room. Its furnishings held no hint of the southwest and would have fitted my London grandmother's townhouse. When I remarked on this, Marguerite explained.

"I was born in England where my father worked for many years. He was a lawyer too and I was seven before we returned to America. I furnished this house like the one that I remembered," she said.

"I stayed in London with relatives last summer. Where did you live?" I asked.

When she told me, I exclaimed, with shocked surprise, "I lived in South Kensington too!"

Learning that fact made me feel close to her though she was long gone from London before I had lived there. But it was like with an old school tie: one can feel delighted to meet a classmate with whom they barely had contact years before.

We both smiled, these being our second real smiles that day.

"Why did you become a lawyer?" I asked.

Marguerite became silent and her face darkened, Harry moved closer and put his arm around her.

"I'm sorry. Have I raised something painful?" I asked.

Marguerite choked up, and it was Harry who answered.

"Marguerite's mother was killed in a robbery and the criminals were never found. Afterward, her father returned to America with her and her brother."

"That's one of the reasons that I became a prosecutor," Marguerite said.

A moment later, the room's heavy silence was shattered by the ringing of the house phone.

Chapter 83

Everyone froze until Marguerite ran to the phone, picked it up, and spoke her name.

"Would you like to speak with Rafael? He's having a wonderful time," the voice said.

"Yes, I would," she said, calmly.

We listened over the speakerphone. You have to give Marguerite credit. She managed to keep herself together.

The conversation between mother and son was brief. Rafael said that he was having a good time and was allowed his favorite snack, the Hostess Twinkies which his mother only rarely permitted him. The man then returned to the phone.

The escape plan that he presented was simple. It sounded familiar, like something from a movie that I saw or a book that I had read. The condemned man would be given a drug to induce heart attack symptoms. He would then be taken to a hospital and pronounced dead. His body would be quickly removed and a waiting hearse would bring him to Mexico for alleged burial in his home town. He would then disappear or perhaps rise from the dead under a new identity.

Marguerite's task was to inform the condemned man of the plan and to smuggle in the drug. During his "medical emergency," she would demand that he be removed to a hospital rather than be treated in the prison's medical unit. This should not be an issue since the ward was not equipped to deal with serious emergencies. These were usually treated at the nearby hospital.

"When will Rafael be released?" Marguerite asked.

"As soon as the hearse enters Mexico, Rafael will be dropped off at his grandmother's home, happy to have met his new uncle. Payment for your service has already been wired to your bank account. We will do business again," came the suave voice.

We sat stunned after Marguerite hung up the phone. The plan seemed sound and might work. But her life would be destroyed either way. If successful, considering the five-million-dollar payment, Marguerite would thereafter be owned by the drug cartel. If the escape plan failed, Rafael would die and she would be arrested once the payment was discovered. And we had no doubt that it would be.

None of us could think of a way out.

"The team will be here soon. That's why our company earns the big bucks," I said, hoping to convey greater confidence than I felt.

Chapter 84

When I was very young and became upset, my mother would say, "Someday this will all be over. This too will pass." But I didn't say this now. What kids had to deal with was nothing like the present situation.

We sat silently, brooding.

"We have to do something!" Marguerite said.

She went online to check her bank balance, fearing what she would find. Sure enough, five-million-dollars had been wired into her bank account ninety minutes earlier.

"I wish that I felt richer," Marguerite said, with a wry smile.

We knew that she would gladly give up everything to be holding Rafael.

"I'd better get back to the hotel, in case Randy gets back early," I said, rising from the sofa.

"I'll drive you," Harry said.

"No, I'll take a taxi. You should be here for when they phone again," I said.

The taxi came quickly and the ride was brief. I was back in my hotel room sooner than I wished. I still hadn't decided what to say to Randy. Maybe I should wait until we were naked in bed. A confrontation then might be more likely to reveal the truth. But it would be a sticky situation.

So I fell back on my original plan: to play things by ear. And, with this decision, I fell asleep.

Margaret in Berlin

I must have been really tired because despite all that had happened that day my sleep was dreamless. The ringing phone awoke me. Randy had forgotten my cell phone number and called the hotel to reach me. This is *not* a good sign, I thought.

"I'll be leaving in about an hour. I thought I'd call and tell you," Randy said.

"Thanks for calling. I was wondering," I said.

"The meeting turned out really well. I made some good contacts," Randy said.

"That's great," I said, in a flat tone.

Silence followed, we both feeling so emotionally blocked that our usual easy banter was gone.

"Are you alright?" he asked finally.

"I'm fine. I just have things on my mind. We'll talk when you get here," I said.

"OK, see you later," Randy said.

"See you," I responded.

I was sure that Randy got my unspoken message. Years before, we had begun *our* tradition: when speaking on the phone. I would address him as "my darling," a phrase that I had picked up from an old movie, and before hanging up we would assure each other of our love.

But not that night.

Chapter 85

My mind was in a muddle. I still hadn't decided what to say. Should I accuse Randy of unfaithfulness as soon as he walked through the door or wait? But was what he had done infidelity? We weren't married and the issue of our being faithful had never arisen. It had merely been my assumption, and possibly the result of poor communication.

Moreover, boys and girls are different. While both have powerful sexual needs, the emotional aspect associated with sex is stronger for a girl. I couldn't have sex with a boy that I didn't love but this might not be the same for most boys.

Hoping to relax, I watched the local TV news. There were the usual reports of the fires and burglaries that occur in every city. But some stories were interesting.

Giant corporations were becoming serious about permitting their employees to work at home. A worker at Dell described how this change had improved her life, and that of her two young children too.

Could it be the same for me? I wondered. The management post for which Vladimir was grooming me didn't demand travel. I could easily do many of the tasks from home, and if I had children...

The second interview more greatly interested me. It was with the former head of the Texas Rangers, wearing a ten-gallon hat and all. He began by describing Texas history and how the Rangers came into being.

"Texas has always been big on order but not so much on law. Many of the state's founders, including Stephen Austin and William Travis, were criminals in the eyes of Mexico.

"After the revolution, the Anglo-Texans desperately needed protection from Indians, Mexicans, and each other. Informal bands of Rangers were established and these became official in 1835. That was before even the government of Texas became official.

"The Rangers needed to be brutal in those days when there was little allegiance to law. Some Rangers were little better than the rustlers they killed.

"Early Texans thought that criminals had forfeited their right to live. In other states they said that if a person does the crime they should be willing to do the time. Here, in Texas, they carried punishment to an extreme.

"But the lawyers and courts weren't much better than the criminals. Formal justice was a joke since many of the accused were related by blood or marriage or business. Things are different now but not completely.

"Philosophically, many Texas Rangers still hold onto the ways of the early days when they shot quickly. Then, the punishment for virtually any crime was death. While no present-day official wants *that*, many of them feel that today's society has lost a crucial insight."

"What's that?" the TV interviewer asked, gazing intently at him.

She was a long-haired, short-skirted, busty woman in her twenties who seemed enthralled by this man.

"That in Texas we recognize that while there is the justice of lawyers and the courtroom, there is also the justice of The Prophets and of God."

I repeated aloud what he had said: "There is the justice of lawyers and the courtroom, and the justice of The Prophets and of God."

Not only Texans believe that, I thought. Vladimir would certainly agree.

I wrote down the man's name. I would invite him to dinner and try to hire him. Vladimir was always seeking good employees and this newly-retired Ranger was definitely his kind of guy.

Chapter 86

As it turned out, I didn't say much to Randy. I simply laid out the evidence on the sofa: the box of condoms with four of them missing. He stared at them, stared at me, and began crying.

"I'm *so* sorry," he wailed.

Well, maybe I should have thrown him out but that's not what I did. Instead, I behaved as have women from age-old times: forgiving him though he didn't deserve it.

I did insist that he tell me what happened since only by understanding why a lover behaved badly can one be sure that it won't happen again. One mistake is acceptable. But two such behaviors would indicate a pattern and Randy's permanent exit from my life.

"I was invited to a party at her house. The punch was spiked. I drank too much and she drank too much and it happened on the floor," Randy said, sheepishly.

Though disapproving, I couldn't help smiling inwardly. Uptight, fearful Randy getting drunk at a party and having sex on the floor. Considering that we had been together for six years, his behavior *was* an ethical mistake but it might have been healthy for his development too.

Moreover, he could no longer choose the high ground when learning of the exploits that I had gotten into. But I had never shared details of these with him. This was partly because of his fearfulness but mostly because secrets remain secret only if they're not revealed.

Margaret in Berlin

I was cautious. I wouldn't be sexually active with Randy, not even kissing him, until I had more facts. Which is what I told him.

"I had planned for Austin to be our pre-marital honeymoon until discovering this. I've never had sex and you say that this girl was the only sexual encounter that you ever had. Is that true?" I asked, in a tell-me-no-nonsense tone.

"No one else, I swear!" Randy burst out.

"You needn't swear. I've known you long enough to know that you're a lousy liar. But we don't know how many men this girl had sex with and I'm thinking in terms of health. Did you use a condom *every* time that you had sex? All four times," I asked.

"We only had sex once. The condoms were hers and my hands shook so badly that they spilled from the box when I opened it. I lost three of them and she told me to keep the box," Randy said.

It was now crystal-clear what had happened. Randy is handsome but shy and he tends attract bossy girls. I had begun making decisions for us soon after we met. Our relationship wouldn't have gotten anywhere if I hadn't.

Randy had gotten drunk, his usual rigid self-control had vanished, and she had pushed herself onto him maybe literally. He should have known better but... I told him my decision.

"Once Randy, *one time* I'll forgive you but *never* again!" I said, firmly.

"Never. I swear!" I know that I haven't been much of a boyfriend because feelings are hard for me. But I do love you," Randy said, almost as a cry.

Margaret in Berlin

I gently covered his mouth with my hand and pulled him close.

"It's late, my darling, and time for us to be in bed," I whispered.

Chapter 87

Sex is like Christmas. Whether it was good or bad, it's hard to describe the experience so I won't try.

Unlike Erika's boyfriend, Clarence, Randy had no sexual difficulty. He even regained his sense of humor. When he asked if he was my best lover, I replied that he was my only lover.

"That's *not* the answer I hoped for. Be honest now, am I not the *best* lover that you've ever had?" he asked.

"Yes, you are," I replied, batting my eyes as I've seen in old-time movies.

"Thank you for your honesty," Randy replied, deadpan, and we burst out laughing.

Then we cuddled, fell asleep, and by morning the troubled past was forgotten.

After breakfast, which was ordered from the hotel's room service, Randy returned to the conference. There was a talk about remote controlled drones that he wanted to attend. It would be given by an expert from DARPA.

"DARPA is the Defense Department's Advanced Research Agency," Randy explained.

I smiled appreciatively though already knowing what DARPA is. Boys like for girls to look up to them. This isn't an issue for me. We all have quirks and if this one helped Randy feel better, it isn't a problem for me and our marriage would be a good one.

After Randy left, I lay around the suite, thinking. Losing my virginity hadn't been a big deal, it seemed. I felt no older or more mature and hadn't learned anything from the experience except how much fun sex could be. Before leaving Austin, I intended for us to spend an entire day in bed. We would order up food and watch TV, like a long-married couple though I wouldn't say that.

But, as is often said, man proposes and God disposes so this never happened. There were more immediate needs: to hire the Texas Ranger, Cody; and to aid in the rescue of a kidnapped child for which, unexpectedly, Randy's assistance proved crucial.

Chapter 88

Cody wasn't hard to locate. I called the TV station, introduced myself as Vladimir's assistant, and was given their contact number for him. But getting through to him took persuasion. Since his interview, he had been besieged by calls offering TV time, book contracts, and even endorsement for a political career. Maybe if I had sounded like a Texas native things would have been easier.

Still, perhaps taking pity at my youthful voice, his wife finally put him through and I made my spiel. I told Cody that I represented my father's international company which provided security and conducted investigations for governments and wealthy individuals.

I received the usual reaction when telling him my father's name: "He's a Russian general," Cody said.

"He's retired from the military and his partners are also retired, from Britain's Secret Intelligence Service and the CIA," I said.

"It sounds like an old fart's club," Cody said.

I couldn't help laughing and heard his wife shush him.

"Vladimir isn't *that* old. We have offices in Berlin and London and will be opening an office in America. Austin is an important city and it could be here. You wouldn't have to travel much.

"I'd like to take you and your wife to dinner to discuss our offer. You choose the restaurant and there are no strings attached. You won't find a better employer," I said.

"What if I want to retire?" Cody asked.

"People like you don't retire. They make others wish that they had," I replied.

Cody laughed and spoke briefly with his wife, He asked where I was staying and, when I told him, said that he would pick me up and I agreed.

Men prefer women who agree with them.

Chapter 89

It didn't surprise me that Cody's car was a Toyota 4Runner. Randy, who is car crazy but a lousy driver, swears that he would buy one when he gets his first job. I simply smile.

What he likes about the car, which is a rugged body-on-frame SUV, is that it has more off-road capability than almost any rival, a strong V6 engine, and a large cargo capacity. There is also an optional third-row seat providing space for more kids than I intend for us to have.

Cody's wife was a surprise. I had imagined her to be a sturdily built, no nonsense type like him but she wasn't. Joanne was small, about 5' 3", a delicate blond with a huge smile. She sat in the back seat with me and we spoke while Cody drove.

"How do you like Austin?" she asked.

"I do. It's different from Greenwich but in good ways. The atmosphere is more relaxed and the people are friendlier. Maybe it was like this during frontier days when everyone came from somewhere else and needed help.

"Greenwich is old money and established. My family's roots go back to just after the Civil War. One ancestor was a Connecticut Chief Justice and my father is a lawyer so we've always fit in, but..."

Cody spoke as Joanne touched my hand.

"I thought that Vladimir was your father," he called from the front seat.

Here we go again, I thought, having to explain my odd background.

"I was adopted at birth and only recently learned that Vladimir is my biological father," I said.

I could have added that I had an English father too but wanted to keep my story simple.

We didn't speak again until after reaching the restaurant but it was a comfortable silence.

My being vegetarian didn't present a problem that evening. The award-winning restaurant that Cody or Joanne had chosen was *Qui* in East Austin. While specializing in meat, there are also enough dishes for a vegetarian to survive on. Or at least one who isn't a rigid vegetarian like me.

Cody said that we should eat before talking business, which was fine with me. The sex seemed to have made me ravenous.

Qui resembles the classic French restaurants where the food's presentation is as important as the food and odd combinations are prized. You might consider chicken liver pate with fried crickets or pork blood and mushrooms enticing but I passed on them.

The restaurant is hipster-like with an open-kitchen area in full view of the diners. The service was superb though the menu was bewildering as to where to begin and end since the visually stunning food was creative too.

I chose the most predictable dishes though even these seemed a bit mysterious: Smoked Ocean Trout seasoned with goat milk, nectarine, white onion, Thai chili, and tomato; Grilled Lettuce (walnut, lemon, artichoke, goat milk curd, and fava beans); Kare Kare (peanut curry and seasonal vegetables). For dessert I chose White Chocolate Mousse.

"You're hungry," Joanne observed, as I ate with gusto.

Margaret in Berlin

"I had a loving night," I blurted.

This was a Freudian slip, I having intended to say "lovely day." My words stopped our conversation and they both smiled. Joanne took Cody's hand and I imagined that she was recalling their youth.

As we awaited the dessert, Cody turned toward me.

"A retired Russian general who lives in Berlin, works with CIA and SIS veterans, and has an American daughter. I like to know the people that I might work with. Tell me about him," Cody ordered.

So that's what I did.

Chapter 90

I thought before replying. How much did I want to reveal? That Vladimir's wartime "take no prisoners" arrogance still persisted?

Decades earlier, when several of his soldiers were kidnapped by Syrian terrorists and the kidnappers were captured, he had ordered them killed with their testicles stuffed in their mouth. Their villages were then burned and no Russian was ever kidnapped again.

Or should I describe how he rescued me from a Tokyo mobster while I lay naked and bound to a table awaiting death by torture?

Nothing of these, I decided, for Cody already knew of the world's horrors. Instead, I spoke in different terms: of Vladimir's nature as a father and an employer.

"Vladimir has an unusual background. He served in Russia's Special Forces and Presidential Security Service. After retiring, he began a security business in Berlin which is really a small private army.

"His company provides protection and other services for government officials and wealthy families. You'll never find a better friend or employer for loyalty is his watchword. But he can also be a person's worst enemy. He believes, as you said on TV, that there is the justice of the lawyers and the courtroom and the justice of The Prophets and of God.

"Vladimir considers an important role of his organization as being to grant God's justice. When I told him of your background and what you had said, he replied that you are both on the side of the angels. I am here to hire you," I said.

Margaret in Berlin

"I've had job offers," Cody said.

His eyes stabbed into mine and I realized that we had begun negotiating.

"None can be as good as ours," I said, with an assured tone.

My English grandmother is very proper. In her youth, she had been presented at Buckingham Palace so she knows good manners. During my summer in London, she had done her best to drill these into me. One of her lessons was that polite people don't discuss salary. Thus, I didn't speak of this or of the other job benefits. Instead, I removed an envelope from my purse and handed it to Cody. It contained a simple one-page contract covering salary, benefits, signing bonus, confidentiality, and the prospect of a future partnership.

"Here is our offer. You won't match it anywhere," I said.

I knew that he couldn't. I had done my homework and our offer was four times his previous government salary. There was also a one-hundred-thousand-dollar signing bonus, a five-thousand-dollar a month expense account, a leased car of his choosing, a leased apartment in Austin (of his choosing) for business meetings or overnight stays, and security upgrades for his home. The usual comprehensive medical insurance and retirement benefits that large corporations provide was also included.

Cody held the sheet so that both he and his wife could read it. Then he returned it to me.

"What about vacation time?" he asked.

"We don't quibble about such matters. As much as you want so long as you get your job done," I said, and Cody nodded.

It hadn't been a serious question. Our offer had overwhelmed him and he felt that he had to say something.

"When do you need an answer?" he asked.

My eyes locked onto his from across the table.

"I apologize for pressuring you but I must have your answer before we leave the restaurant. There's a situation that our company is currently handling. It involves the kidnapping of a Texas politician's son," I replied.

I handed him a pen, and Cody looked toward his wife.

"I don't want you laying around the house upsetting my routine," she said, in a mock stern tone.

Cody nodded, signed the contract, and returned it to me. I counter-signed it and handed him the bonus check that I had written earlier.

"When do I start work?" he asked me.

I smiled and extended my hand which he grasped firmly.

"You just have," I said.

Chapter 91

Cody never could have tolerated retirement. He was eager to begin working and I filled him in.

"It's sticky. A child has been abducted by a drug cartel. For his safe return, they demand that their boss be released from Texas' Death Row," I said.

"The governor will never do it," Cody said.

"I agree, but their plan isn't for him to know. They want the child's mother to help him escape."

"Does she work at the prison?"

"No. She's the Texas Attorney General," I replied.

Cody and Joanne exhaled deeply as their eyes riveted on my face.

"That is a problem. What have you done so far?" Cody asked, calmly.

"The kidnappers first made contact yesterday. As proof of life, they're having the child phone home daily. He believes that he's staying with his uncle who is letting him play video games as long as he wants and provides endless snacks. He's having a ball.

"Our team consists of former Special Forces and a retired FBI agent and arrives tomorrow. I know someone local who can obtain whatever equipment is needed. They're the best but we really need you," I said.

"That's far too many bosses. Who's in charge?" Cody asked.

"You are. I'll tell them when they arrive. If anyone gives you pushback, send them to me," I said firmly.

"Yes ma'am," Cody said.

"In this company we're all on a first-name basis," I said.

"Yes, Margaret, yes boss-lady," he said, with a small smile.

Joanne squeezed his hand and smiled too.

That was the moment when my life permanently changed though there would be others. That evening, during a fabulous meal in Austin, I became a boss and would never look back.

Chapter 92

The team arrived early the next morning. They had come on a private plane and slept most of the way. I had intended to give them a few hours to rest but this wasn't necessary.

There were five of them: four men and a woman. The men were tall and sturdily built with short-cut hair. They looked like they belonged in uniform. Apart from the American, the other men, judging by their accent, appeared to be Russian. The woman might have been British or had been educated in England.

Vladimir had faxed me their names but I introduced them as Bill, Will, Ted, Len, and Jill. Their real names were unimportant and they wouldn't have wanted them to be known. The only thing that counted was they being good at their jobs. I knew that they must be if they worked for us.

I scheduled our first planning meeting at Cody's house, fearing that Harry and Marguerite's house might be watched by the kidnappers.

As the team relaxed with drinks and snacks, I provided introductions before getting down to business. I described the kidnapper's demands and that they couldn't be agreed to.

"Why not? What's the value of a drug dealer? They're quickly replaced," Ted asked.

I looked toward Cody.

"It's American policy not to pay ransom, and Texans demand the death penalty for convicted murderers," he said.

"The state has no flexibility?" Jill asked.

"Not with that monster," Cody replied.

"You're saying that Rafael must die!" Marguerite said, heatedly.

Cody didn't reply as silence settled over the room.

"No, he's not saying that. Texans have a history of putting aside rules and laws when lives are endangered. Isn't that so, Cody?"

"Yes, Margaret," he agreed, nodding.

"So we now have two important goals, both of which must be met: Rafael's rescue, and the execution of a killer. Do we agree?" I asked.

There were nods about the room but no one spoke.

"It doesn't matter *how* the prisoner dies so long as he dies. Wouldn't you agree?" I asked.

I was leading the group toward accepting my plan.

Again, there were no objections.

"So the prisoner will escape, Rafael will return home, and Marguerite's Mexican relatives will be relocated here. *All* before we execute the legally condemned murderer," I said.

What surprised me, after I spoke these words, was how self-possessed I felt. I was wholly without discomfort or embarrassment at what I had proposed. I was certainly Vladimir's daughter, as others had been insisting for years.

Later, while Marguerite relaxed and I helped Joanne clean-up in the kitchen, she took me aside.

"Cody just gave you his rarest compliment," she said.

"What was that?"

Margaret in Berlin

"He said that you were a real Texan," Joanne replied.

Chapter 93

I had behaved as Vladimir had instructed me and it worked. "Treat your employees with confidence and warmth but don't be afraid of confrontation," he said.

I had become their boss and they trusted me. Now all that we could do was to await the kidnapper's call. Which must come soon for the execution would be in sixteen days.

Jill returned with Harry and Marguerite to their home. If it were being watched, a woman who looked as sexy as Jill would seem no threat. None but me knew of her deadly history and expertise with both knife and pistol. She wore a knife strapped to her thigh while a pistol lay in a waistband holster.

It was still early when I returned to the hotel. Randy wouldn't be back for at least several hours so, after getting the extra robe that we needed from the concierge, I turned toward the hotel's bar to hang-out. A skyscraper was being built on the street that our room faced. There, it was too noisy to think. I could have demanded another room but had more important things on my mind.

I sat at a table at the rear of the bar. When the waiter arrived, I ordered a club soda with a twist of lime and a plate of almonds.

My plan, though sounding simple, was anything but. We could not just enable a condemned prisoner's escape even if his body were quickly found. An official investigation was inevitable, the first of many. How well would Marguerite, who would have been one of the prisoner's last visitors, hold up under questioning? If threatened with indictment and the loss of her child, she might choose to turn us in.

Margaret in Berlin

No, we needed official sanction for our actions. I hoped for Cody to obtain this in Texas and for Vladimir to obtain Washington's approval if our operation spread into Mexico.

I sprawled on the comfortable leather chair and sipped my drink. Much of its fizzle was gone as were my ideas. Nothing arose from my drained mind. I didn't notice the man until he sat opposite me.

"Would you mind company?" he asked.

Chapter 94

I gave the man a cool, uninterested look.

"My fiancée is late. He's bigger than you and tends to be jealous," I said.

"I'm not looking for a pickup, just conversation," he said.

Now I studied him closely. He was in his thirties and, though casually dressed, his clothes were obviously expensive. His hair and mustache were neatly trimmed and his nails were clean. But despite the moderate temperature of the room, he was shaking as if chilled.

"Have I passed inspection?" he asked, genially.

"Are you staying here?" I asked, returning his question with mine.

"Temporarily, until things get sorted out. I was carjacked twenty minutes ago," he said.

That statement got me sitting up straight. If I had just been robbed, I would have needed someone to talk to too.

"Are you hurt?" I asked, sympathetically.

"Just my pride that it happened so fast. I was shown a gun, my wallet and car were demanded, and I instantly obeyed. No car is worth your life though I did love it. It was a new Camaro and I had just washed it," he said.

"My father loves his too. His first car was a Camaro," I said.

At this point the waiter arrived. He looked at the man and threw me an unspoken question to which I nodded that things were OK.

"You've had a really bad day. The least that one could do is to buy you a drink. What will you have?" I asked.

"That's very good of you but just club soda. I'm Mormon and we don't drink," he said.

"Mine is club soda. I'm Mormon too," I said, with a real grin and sense of comradeship.

It was like meeting a school chum years after graduation, when both resurrect the old school bond.

"Are you down from Utah?" he asked.

"No, I'm a long way from there: Greenwich, Connecticut," I replied.

"Not many Mormons there."

"No, but my mother's goal is conversion so maybe someday," I said, with a smile.

"You're not religious," he said.

This was more a statement than a question. His conclusion had probably derived from my comment that I was traveling with my fiancée. Mormons don't approve of premarital sex.

"I'm a Barnard student. When living at home, I attend church every Sunday," I said.

After several moments of comfortable silence, I asked the typical American question: "What kind of work do you do?"

Before he answered, a strange thing happened. He calmed and his shaking stopped. A light seemed to steal across his frozen face which had relaxed and appeared transformed, as if a moment of self-revelation had occurred perhaps from the recent trauma.

The words he spoke were melodramatic but his eyes bore into mine and I didn't doubt their truth. They also sounded a bit crazy but in a hallowed way, the type of madness that advances individuals, and nations too.

"I've been a criminal lawyer for twelve years. Before this evening, like most lawyers, I accepted cases irrespective of the defendant's guilt so long as their crimes didn't cross my path. But this evening changed me. I now feel that I must war against the criminal. I must become a hunter of evil," he said.

Chapter 95

A popular saying is that providence watches over the deserving. If so, Harry and Marguerite fit within that category. This is relevant because had Clinton, the man that I met that evening, not been robbed, it is unlikely that we would have met. Then Rafael would probably have died but who can say for sure? Another popular saying is that fate is fickle.

I retrieved a business card from my purse and handed it to Clinton.

"One who tries to avoid their fate is both a coward and a fool. My father's international security company is always seeking intelligent, moral people with a backbone. Those who would act outside the conventional but on the side of the angels. We battle for causes which others believe lost but are worth fighting for," I said.

"And how do you know that I'd fit in?" Clinton asked, after a long stare.

"My sense or instinct, call it what you will. But lawyers are cautious and don't make impulsive decisions. You must check us out but this shouldn't take long with the Internet. Do you live nearby? How will you get home?" I asked.

"I'm not sure. I live in Rollingwood, about six miles outside Austin. My wife is away, visiting her mother in Salt Lake City. It's embarrassing not to have money. This has been another new experience for me," he said, with a deprecating smile.

"We can't have that," I said.

My tone had been maternal despite he being far older. I reached into my purse and took from my wallet two one-hundred dollar bills.

"This should get you home. If you feel too shaken-up to travel, tell the concierge that you're our company's guest. You'll be a business expense for a potential employee," I said, matter-of-factly.

I was following Vladimir's orders. He had told me not to be stingy when doing business.

There was a long hesitation before he accepted the money.

"I don't know how to thank you. I'll pay you back," he said.

"Forget it. Someday, I may need a favor," I said, with a shrug.

Two uniformed policeman and two men dressed in suits, who were probably detectives, strode toward our table as Clinton handed me his card.

"Are you alright, sir?" the older detective asked.

"I'm fine, just a little shaken up," Clinton replied.

"We'd prefer to learn the details of your robbery in private," the detective said, glancing at me.

I rose and extended my hand, which Clinton took.

"Until we meet again," he said, with a smile.

"Until we meet again," I repeated.

Four police officers don't quickly arrive after a robbery in which the victim isn't injured. Clinton must be an important person, I thought.

Before leaving, I asked the concierge, "Who is Clinton Dewberry?"

"You don't know?"

"No."

"He's Clyde Dewberry's son."

"Who's Clyde Dewberry?" I asked.

The waiter stared at me as if I came from another planet. My Eastern accent had given me such looks since I arrived in Texas.

"He's dead but was a much-beloved lieutenant-governor for years. He made a fortune in the oil and gas industry."

Chapter 96

We waited: Marguerite, Harry, and the team for a phone call; me, for Randy's arrival; and maybe Clinton, for a taxi or a room. So I phoned home, which is what people usually do when they feel antsy.

After my mother picked up, I told her what she wanted to hear: that I had arrived in Austin safely and was having a peaceful time. Of course I said nothing about Randy or Rafael's kidnapping. Although my mother approved of non-Mormon/irreligious Randy as my fiancée, she didn't support pre-marital sex or my participation in risky work.

She respected Vladimir and acknowledged that he was my biological father but his having an out-of-wedlock child with a live-in girlfriend while being married turned her off.

Still, my old-fashioned mother was a good woman and would applaud my helping Clinton if she knew. She was considered an angel by our neighbors, but might be too angelic for today's world, Randy had observed.

Yet, my mother had reared her daughters well for we all possessed the essence of good breeding: good temper, easy flippancy, alert manners, and an indifference to good looks. Despite our disagreements, I always missed her.

My younger sisters told me of their latest dilemmas: no longer liking a boy that they once liked, and being less popular than they were in their last grade. But it was the story of my oldest sister's latest date that lingered in my mind after hanging up.

Melody had agreed to meet a man that she met on Tinder after discovering that they both loved movies. Though now working as a para-legal before attending law school, her long-term goal is to be a film critic. She plans to use her law degree as an entrée into the entertainment industry.

She and twenty-four-year-old Bradley had met at a trendy bar in Manhattan's East Village. Like most Mormons, Melody doesn't drink but she also doesn't try to impose her views on others.

After sharing movie memories, Bradley got down to his hobby which seemed to be downing as many Gin and Tonics as quickly as possible. Soon, he tried to stand to go to the bathroom but stumbled. As he turned to hand Melody something, he looked sick. She asked if he was OK, his cheeks filled with vomit, and it sputtered onto her and the floor. She helped him home and refused his invitation for pillow-talk.

Being an older sister, Melody feels that it is her duty to end each of her personal stories with a moral. This one I'll always remember: "No matter how terrible you think a date is, so long as it doesn't end with vomit on your heels there's still hope though maybe not enough for a second date."

My thinking instantly turned to Randy and our marriage someday. I *hoped* that my dating life was over.

Chapter 97

Randy returned at a little after 8:00PM. It was while we were kissing that my phone rang.

"The kidnapper called and our team is meeting in twenty minutes. I'll pick you up," Cody said abruptly.

"I have to go," I told Randy.

He had been kissing my neck with his hands exploring my groin when I made this statement. Naturally, he was a bit upset.

"Now, at this minute?" he asked.

"I'm sorry. I'm helping Vladimir with an emergency. I'll be back as soon as I can, my darling," I said, disengaging from his embrace.

"Who are you meeting?" he asked suspiciously.

He's afraid that I'm having an affair, I thought.

"It *is* a man but he's a retired Texas Ranger, happily married and three times our age. Come downstairs and you can meet him," I said.

Randy is shy at meeting strangers so I didn't expect for him to take up my offer but he did. As we waited in the hotel lobby, I told him a few details. Enough that he would trust me but not so many that he would worry.

"I can tell you a little but you must promise never to speak of it for lives are at stake," I said.

"I never tell anyone anything that you tell me," he said, a bit angrily.

"I'm sorry, but I'm nervous. I don't doubt you," I said, apologetically, before continuing.

"A child has been kidnapped and Vladimir's company is trying to rescue him. I'm his representative on the ground, coordinating things. Word was just gotten from the kidnappers and we're having this emergency meeting," I said.

"Will you be in danger?" Randy asked.

"Not at all. We're meeting at the Ranger's home. I'll be as safe as if I were in Greenwich," I said, reassuringly.

"That's not quite reassuring. I don't want to lose you," Randy said.

He was referring to the risky Greenwich events that I had been embroiled in, and our recent fight.

"I'll be fine, my darling," I said, closing this conversation with a kiss.

Randy held me tight until Cody arrived. I introduced them.

"So you're the computer-genius boyfriend," he said, gripping Randy's hand and clasping his shoulder warmly.

"Well, you might say that," Randy replied shyly.

Randy doesn't take praise well.

Cody turned toward me.

"We could use a computer expert," he said, tellingly.

My employee is seeking the permission of the boss lady, I told myself, with more than a little satisfaction.

Chapter 98

I looked at Randy uncertainly, feeling unsure of exactly who he is for only the second time in our long relationship. The first was the previous day when I learned that he had cheated on me.

Randy is a wonderful boy: thoughtful, responsible, hard-working and, until recently, I had believed him to be faithful. But he had vowed *that* fault was over and I believed him.

In any case, sexual faithfulness was irrelevant to the task that we faced. Intelligence wasn't and Randy is a genius with computers. I wasn't his mother and not yet his wife so the decision to join us must be his alone.

"We need you. Will you work with us?" I asked Randy.

His response surprised me for it lacked his usual hesitancy.

"I wouldn't miss it," he said, grinning.

We held hands on the brief ride to Cody's home. There, I introduced him to the others as "Randy, our computer expert." That he was my boyfriend didn't matter.

The drug that Marguerite needed would be delivered by UPS to her home. To be effective, it must be injected into a muscle and Marguerite would have to do the injecting. How this could be accomplished with a condemned prisoner under continual guard presented a problem for which I had no answer.

"A power outage," Randy suggested, and all eyes turned toward him.

"There'll be a delay and blackout until the backup generators kick in but they won't be able to handle everything. Prison doors may open but there'll be chaos even if they don't. Marguerite will have her chance then," Randy said, with a smile.

I sat open-mouthed as the others stared at him with amazement. But why am I surprised? Randy *is* a genius, I reminded myself.

"How can this be done?" Cody asked.

"Their electrical system must be computerized. I'll need the name of the company handling it and will hack into their system. It shouldn't be difficult with the help of someone that I met at the conference I'm attending," Randy said.

"What you'll be doing isn't legal. Can they be trusted?" I asked.

If we failed and were arrested, I didn't want Randy part of *that* equation. I trusted that he would visit me regularly in jail.

"I won't tell him what he's working on and he'll be leaving the country once the conference is over. He's a Russian nerd and his English isn't the best. I doubt that he pays attention to American news. He'll never know what happened," Randy answered, with another smile.

"Alyosha survives financially by doing free-lance hacking for the Russian Mafia. He'll expect to be paid," Randy said.

"How much?" I asked.

"He told me that his biggest fee was the equivalent of twenty-thousand dollars."

"Tell him that we'll pay him thirty-thousand dollars, half up-front and the rest when the work is completed to your satisfaction. Get his bank wiring instructions where to send the money," I instructed Randy, who grinned.

"What?" I asked.

"His name, Alyosha. It means 'one who helps people,'" Randy replied.

"We'll need more than that: implicit approval from both the state and federal governments for our actions. Freeing Rafael and having his parents wind up in jail is no solution," Cody said.

"I couldn't agree more," I said.

Then I told them about *my* helpers.

Chapter 99

Cody, Harry, and Marguerite knew who Clyde Dewberry was. A lieutenant-governor for many years, his death was still mourned. Though a mogul, he had stood up for the little guy. Hospitals and libraries throughout Texas had received bequests in his will.

I told the group about his son, Clinton, who I had recently met, and of the possibility that he would join us.

"His name should carry weight in the state government, and one of our Board members was a highly ranked CIA official. The Justice Department will listen to him. Besides, exactly what are we proposing: to rescue a kidnapped child and carry out a lawful execution. How could any reasonable official object to that?"

"Unless it goes wrong and the condemned man escapes," Cody said.

"So nothing must go wrong," I said.

I turned toward Randy.

"What do you know about Alyosha?" I asked.

"Well, he *is* a crook but he's also very smart. I'm trying to convince him to return with me to Yale. My advisor would hire him after their five-minute conversation.

"Alyosha's lecture to the conference concerned how our lives will change in the latest age of machines. Some human tasks are incredibly difficult for machines. A ten-dollar gadget can beat us at chess but still can't learn by itself.

"What Alyosha has begun working on, all by himself since he's a loner, is *deep* learning modeled on the human brain. It can teach machines to ignore all but the important characteristics of something and will open the door to driverless cars and medical diagnosis better than doctors can do. Think about just one advance: a world where driverless cars and trucks will be faster, more efficient, and safer than error-prone human drivers. And that's just the start."

When Randy gets enthusiastic he can talk for hours. Now he had forgotten why we were here, becoming engrossed in his love of computers which I hoped would always remain secondary to me.

I interrupted him.

"You've convinced us. How soon can you bring Alyosha onboard?" I asked him.

"He won't talk on the phone. He doesn't trust them from hacking. I'll see him as soon as I leave. He's a night owl," Randy replied.

"I'll go with you. If he's to join us, I want a look at him," Cody said.

"OK. We'll meet again in the morning, here at 10AM. I'll speak with Vladimir before then," I said.

Before leaving, I noted Marguerite's troubled face.

"We'll get Rafael back," I said softly, touching her shoulder and speaking with greater assurance than I felt.

She gave a weak smile.

Chapter 100

I arrived back at the hotel at a little after 10PM, having stopped for pancakes at an IHOP with Harry and Marguerite. I wasn't hungry but they didn't want to be alone at home. They gave me a choice among the restaurants that we drove passed and I chose the IHOP. Its Disney-like character appeared the most cheerful.

The lingering thought of missing Rafael had worn them down and hung over us. But eating tends to reduce anxiety and everyone likes pancakes.

This was my first visit to an IHOP and I chose the most Eastern selection: New York Cheesecake Pancakes which is a stack of four buttermilk pancakes loaded with cheesecake pieces, strawberries, powdered sugar, and whipped topping. Guaranteed to go straight to one's hips, I thought.

Marguerite chose the sugar-high Red Velvet Pancakes: super-sweet Red Velvet pancakes topped with cream cheese icing and dusted with powdered sugar.

Harry chose what might be considered the healthiest dish. His pancakes were topped with peaches without the added raspberry and whipped toppings.

To remove our minds from the inescapable, I asked Marguerite about her legal work. This wasn't an idle question. My father is a lawyer and nearly all of our family's dinner conversations concern his work for a few minutes.

I also had time to kill before I could courteously phone Vladimir. Berlin time is six hours ahead of Texas time but it was still too early there.

My asking Marguerite about her job turned out to be a bad idea. Fearing for Rafael, it was probably natural that her mind had turned to death.

"It's ironic. Though opposed to the death penalty, I'm continually being forced to defend it," Marguerite said.

I shared her opinion but not completely. Though Kimberly, a Barnard classmate, had been falsely accused of murder a year earlier, I still felt that some people deserved execution. Which is what I said.

"What about the real monsters? Those who have murdered repeatedly and committed atrocious crimes. Would you defend their right to live?" I asked.

My mind turned to Olga in Berlin, whose life had become dedicated to killing the man that kidnapped her and sold her children. I would help if she asked.

"You might not say that after witnessing an execution. I attended one, feeling that I should since I was responsible for them."

I didn't want to hear the details but couldn't have stopped her. She was on an emotional roll.

Chapter 101

"I received a letter from a man who was executed after his death. This happened two years ago but I still remember what he wrote. 'I must be dead if you are reading this. I enjoyed talking to you. You're a sweet person and I'm sorry that we didn't meet under different circumstances. Thank you for being kind. Have a blessed life.'"

Marguerite's voice trailed off and she took another sip of coffee.

"The executions are done in Huntsville, in an olden prison. It has thirty-foot high walls topped with razor wire. A red brick building holds the death chamber.

"A rigid process is followed. After the condemned man's last meal in his holding cell, he walks to the death chamber a few feet away. There, guards strap him to a gurney with leather belts and IVs are inserted into his arms. Two people remain in the chamber with the inmate: the prison chaplain, and the warden who directs the executioner when to begin.

"Three drugs are injected into the IVs: first, an anesthetic; then, a muscle relaxant; finally, the drug that stops their heart. If all work well, the person seems merely to fall asleep.

I looked at Harry. His face was pale and he had stopped eating. He had obviously heard this before.

"I support the death penalty. I believe some crimes are so awful that you must pay with your life. But I also feel that some who were executed didn't deserve it.

"I can still picture the old woman who arrived for her son's execution. She moved closer to see better through the large pane of glass that separated her from the death chamber. There, lay her son who had been sentenced for the rape and murder of a ten-year-old girl. Her duct-taped, strangled body was found in the trunk of a car.

"The woman's wrinkled hands had pressed to the thick glass. She watched intently as her son's body went limp. While driving home, my face became wet with tears.'

Now, Marguerite faced me directly.

"Though being opposed to the death penalty, I want the prisoner *and* Rafael's kidnappers to die," she said, in a hoarse voice.

Our pancakes lay untouched as I dried my tears with a napkin.

Margaret in Berlin

Chapter 102

The flight was brief. By air, Las Vegas isn't very far from Austin. Randy had wanted to accompany us but I begged him not to. It wasn't a demand for I didn't have the right to ask. He had been involved with the operation since its beginning and had earned the right to witness its ending.

But I had feared the effect that this experience would have on him and he agreed. Sometimes, not always but sometimes, a woman does know what is best for her man.

We flew first-class on American Airlines. It was a late evening, weekday flight and the plane was only half-full. Cody ordered bourbon but the rest of us—Harry, Marguerite, and me—settled for water and bags of pretzels.

Vladimir had once told me to always have a backup plan in case things go wrong. Thankfully, nothing did. Marguerite had visited the prison using the excuse of possibly gaining information from the condemned man in exchange for his life. His lawyer had earlier informed him of the escape, and the prison blackout lasted long enough for Marguerite to inject the drug. She had practiced this on a grapefruit.

The drug didn't take effect until she was gone. The prisoner fainted and couldn't be revived. He was taken to the local hospital where he was believed to have died.

A hearse took him to his hometown for burial. When it passed the border into Mexico, Rafael was released and our team convoyed him and all of his Mexican relatives to safety in America.

But we couldn't have done this alone. Vladimir had called in favors, his CIA partner called in favors, and Clinton called in favors. The Air Force also became involved.

Margaret in Berlin

The hearse had been tracked by a drone since it left the prison: down Sam Houston Avenue in Huntsville, past Laredo and the World Trade Bridge into Monterrey, destined for the town of Aguascalientes, just north of Guadalajara.

Marguerite wanted to witness the final scene and permission was granted. The room that we entered was in the Nevada desert. It was frigidly air-conditioned. The only light came from the glow of computer monitors, and the air smelled of sweat and cigarettes and air-freshener.

The operator zoomed the camera on the hearse. He knew nothing of the condemned man, neither his name nor his deed. He had only been told that the vehicle's inhabitants represented a threat to the United States and were therefore legitimate targets.

The operator hadn't told us his name and none of us asked. He wore a regulation green Air Force suit. Through the chain of command came the order that led to his headset. We sat watching.

The operator switched from the visible TV spectrum to the sharp contrast of infrared. The hearse's heat signature stood out ghostly white against the cool black earth.

A safety observer loomed behind the operator to certify that the weapon's release was correct. There was a long verbal checklist until the targeting laser locked onto the vehicle. Then came the countdown: "Five, four, three, two, one, missile off the rail."

Eighteen hundred miles away, a Predator Drone's Hellfire missile flared to life, detaching from its mount and reaching its maximum speed in seconds. The targeting laser was kept trained on the hearse and we stared intently. Seconds seemed to slow until the screen lit up with white flame.

Margaret in Berlin

We stared until the screen dimmed. Then Harry put his arm around his wife and spoke.

"Come, love, it's time to go home."

Chapter 103

I sat beside Cody on the flight back to Austin.

"Randy didn't come," Cody said, in a statement that was more a question.

"No, I begged him not to. He's sensitive and couldn't take the aftershock," I said.

"You're hardier than him," Cody said, after a brief silence.

I replied without facing him. I had been staring out the window at the black sky.

"Just when I have to be," I said.

"Huh," he grunted.

Cody leaned back and appeared to doze off. I picked up an issue of *Teen Vogue* that someone had left. A story on its cover grabbed my attention: "Blurred Lines: When Teachers Seduce Students." Several of my high school friends had fit into this category. The writer said nothing new, only that this behavior was criminal and accepting a teacher's advance was a big mistake.

I sighed and returned the magazine to the seat rack.

"*What?*" Cody asked, though his eyes remained closed.

"A magazine article about dumb girls who have sex with their teacher," I replied.

"We've had those arrests," Cody said

This was his last comment until he was driving me back to the hotel.

"I have a present for you before you leave Austin. It's in the manila envelope in the seat pocket," Cody said.

The envelope contained a letter addressed to me and a Sheriff's badge.

"A Texas Ranger must be capable of handling any situation without definite instructions from their boss. I couldn't get you appointed a Ranger but the Austin Sheriff is a good friend. You're being appointed a Reserve Deputy Sheriff, fully authorized to carry a weapon and make arrests. I'd hold off on arresting anyone since that power applies only when you're called to active duty."

"Are you *serious?*" I asked, smiling.

"Absolutely," Cody replied, as his gaze remained on the road. "You've been appointed under Section 85.004 of the Texas Local Government Code governing Reserve Deputies. I've given the Sheriff the two-thousand-dollars needed for your bond. You'll be given the oath of office tomorrow at 1:00PM. Afterward, we party," Cody ordered.

I said nothing. I just nodded and grinned. I was Cody's boss but would follow this order. And though it might seem silly, I felt as happy as a child who had finally been given a hungered for toy.

Chapter 104

Things are done differently in Texas. Here, my oath of office wasn't taken in a government building but at a classy shooting range. It wasn't as luxuriously furnished as the range in Greenwich that Erika regularly drags me to but it wasn't redneck bar style either.

The chairs were well-cushioned and the air-conditioning was frigid. The range had high-intensity LED lighting, an acoustic design that reduced noise to near outdoor level, and air management to eliminate lead contaminant from the ammunition fired. Its design exceeded safety standards, the placard on the wall said.

The ceremony was held in the Range's office with me, Randy, Cody, and the Sheriff attending. The team had already left for Berlin. Harry and Marguerite wouldn't leave Rafael's side for a moment and his presence wouldn't have been suitable here though he would have loved it.

Randy grinned as I was being sworn in. After handing me my badge, the Sheriff, with a smile toward Cody, said that deputies must be proficient with firearms and he led me to the firing range.

I acted dumb as he checked that the ear-muffs and protective eyewear that I had put on fit properly. It's always best to have people underestimate you.

The range had twelve firing positions, each being four-foot-wide and seventy-five-foot long.

"Have you ever fired a gun?" the Sheriff asked me.

"I'm a Barnard student. Just a few times at a range in Greenwich," I replied, casually.

"Then we'll begin with a low power weapon. It has little recoil so you needn't be afraid. This is a Sig Sauer .380 Semi-Automatic pistol. It holds seven rounds. I'll show you its safety features and how to load it. Then I'll fire a magazine," he said.

After instructing me, the Sheriff assumed a firing position. Downrange, a paper target showed a masked man pointing a pistol. The Sheriff retrieved it after his seventh shot. Three had hit the man's heart, one had hit his shoulder, two had hit his stomach, and one was a miss.

"Good shooting," Cody said.

I said nothing as the Sheriff handed me the pistol to load.

The Greenwich pistol instructor had extensive experience in the military and state police. I and Erika had been apt pupils. After her mother and sister were raped and murdered by a business enemy of her billionaire father, he had arranged for her bodyguard and self-defense training.

We were taught three shooting stances and told their pros and cons. I found the Weaver position, which is also called the "fighting stance," to be the most comfortable. Here, the shooter's feet are shoulder width apart with the firing side foot being slightly behind the support side foot. The knees are flexed to absorb recoil and the shooter leans slightly forward, holding his arms straight out as he brings the gun sights to his eyes. His head is kept level to maintain balance.

I assumed this position and fired, the first shot slowly but the rest in rapid sequence. Five of my shots hit the bullseye over the mugger's heart and two hits were between his eyes.

"*Excellent shooting,*" Cody boomed, as the Sheriff stared at the retrieved target.

"Let's see how well you do with a *real* weapon," the Sheriff said.

This pistol was a .40 caliber Smith & Wesson, which also held seven shots. The Sheriff didn't explain this weapon's characteristics. He just handed it to me along with a box of ammunition. The target was replaced with a fresh one.

I loaded the magazine and inserted it into the gun. After racking the chamber, I assumed the shooting stance. I hit the target with all seven shots: four were to the heart, two were between the eyes, and the last hit the groin.

"You went low with your last shot," the Sheriff said, after examining the target closely.

"It was deliberate," I replied, demurely, as I returned the weapon to him.

Outside, before leaving the range, the Sheriff took my arm.

"Call me first when you're looking for a job. You're a gifted shot," he said.

"She should be. Her father is a retired Special Forces general," Cody said, grinning.

Thankfully, he didn't say in which nation's army. *That* fact would have raised questions.

Chapter 105

Marguerite, Harry, and their son joined us for the party. The Sheriff was invited but he begged off when a police emergency developed.

In respect of my vegetarianism, Cody had reserved a small room at a vegan restaurant that was open only five hours a day, for lunch and dinner. When we arrived at a little after 3PM, the door was locked. Cody knocked and it was opened by the smiling owner. It was obvious that Cody had pull with her and he promised to tell us the story someday.

Though the food was perfect for me, it wasn't the restaurant that I would have chosen for a party. Others might be put off by the mock meat and chicken, even with the added attraction of drinking fluoride-free water.

But all of us found something to enjoy. I had Freeto Burrito. This is organic tempeh chili, vegan cheese, and avocado wrapped in a grilled tortilla.

Marguerite, Harry, and Randy followed Cody's lead: Mock Chicken Wrap (avocado, sprouts, carrots and soy "chicken" salad wrapped in a grilled tortilla). A Chili Dawg with vegan cheese satisfied Rafael.

Conversation was kept light. Cody told a story about the robber who gave a holdup note to a bank teller. It was written on the back of his company's stationary. Harry told a funny story about a hotel guest, and I spoke of Greenwich. Randy and I would be returning the next day.

"You really haven't seen Austin and must come back," Harry said.

"We will," I promised, for both Randy and me.

Though speaking for him too, I hadn't yet raised the crucial matter underlying why I had accompanied him to Austin: to convince him to accompany me Berlin. I *must* raise this issue tonight, I told myself, making a mental note.

Tonight was a little before ten when we were in bed. The tiny black bra and thong that I wore indicated my mood. I caught Randy's hand as he finished peeling these off.

"In a moment but first we must talk, my darling. I'm spending next semester at a university in Berlin and want you with me," I said.

Randy's hand stopped moving. He sat up and faced me.

"You're asking me to go to Berlin. To attend school there and live with you?" he asked.

"I already checked. The school is famous for its medical and computer programs and Yale would give you credit so you'd graduate on time. I don't want us ever apart," I said, staring into his eyes.

I held my breath as the silence seemed to extend into an eternity. Change isn't easy for Randy.

"Of course I'll come, love. And if my father throws me out, I'll get a computer job to support us," he said.

Then Randy turned out the light and we got down to business.

Chapter 106

I packed for both of us after Randy returned to the conference. It was winding down but he wanted to talk with another speaker.

"To learn something to make me more employable, if the worst happens with my parents," he said.

I smiled and kissed him but doubted that situation would arise. Despite his father's rigidity, he loved his son and wouldn't risk a break. Moreover, Randy was close with his baby sister, and their mother was more flexible.

With this chore completed, I looked around the room for the last time. Much had changed in my life since I arrived. My future career with Vladimir had solidified and my marriage to Randy seemed assured. Nothing can go wrong, I told myself, though recognizing that, too often, this is more prayer than reality.

Still, Randy had chosen his allegiance and it was to me and not his parents. He had finally freed himself from their control. But they'll gain a daughter and not lose a son, as the saying goes.

Soon after we boarded the plane, Randy dozed off in the comfortable First Class cabin. Our heads lay together and we held hands. I felt fully relaxed for the first time since we had arrived in Austin.

While beginning to doze, I remembered the previous night and became moist. We'll have thousands such nights, I told myself, and smiled. Then, recognizing that the vibration I felt was distant from my vagina, I retrieved my phone from my pocket being careful not to wake Randy.

Margaret in Berlin

Erika's capitalized text message was brief: PAMELA MISSING. CALL ME ASAP.

Margaret in Berlin

Chapter 107

"ASAP" was three hours later when our flight landed at Newark Airport. Despite the storm, which played havoc with phone reception, we managed to make it on-time. I felt guilty about not replying to Erika's text more quickly and gave her my explanation before she exploded.

"There was a storm and I couldn't call. Our plane just landed. What's up?" I asked.

My tone was casual, knowing of Erika's talent for managing crises. Her tone was now calm. The emergency involving Pamela had either passed or been handled.

"Things were crazy. Pamela ditched her bodyguard and we've been in crisis mode," Erika said.

"Huh," I replied.

Though having helped Pamela to flee her abusive husband and gain temporary sanctuary at Erika's home, Pamela wasn't a relative or even a friend. I had simply done a good deed, and gained goodwill with British officialdom for Vladimir's business too. Pamela was an adult and if she had decided to go off on her own, so be it. Which is what I said.

"It's not that simple. The FBI has nearly moved in with us and Scotland Yard arrives tomorrow. Being a British official gives her father clout. My father has business meetings in his home office, and I have studying. Pamela is sweet but maybe dumb too. How did we ever get involved with her?" Erika asked.

Erika and I are like sisters and she was being tactful. She might have said, "I shouldn't have let you talk me into doing her a favor."

I ignored Erika's fury. There was a problem to face and responding to her justified anger wouldn't be constructive.

"When was she last seen? How did she ditch her bodyguard?" I asked.

"An hour before I texted you. One minute she was in a store trying on bras and the next minute she was gone. She should have had a female bodyguard," Erika replied, in a critical tone.

"Most bodyguards are men. It takes time to set up something special," I said, defending the company that I would someday manage.

"I know and I'm not blaming Vladimir. I'm upset and want everything normal again," Erika said.

Which, a few hours later and without effort on anyone's part, is how they were.

Chapter 108

"It's good that the FBI is gone. It did nothing for my father's business image to have them lounging about his home," Erika said.

"I get that. So what happened?" How come they left?" I asked.

I sank back into the plush chaise lounge as Erika lay exhausted on her bed.

"It never was a crisis. Pamela was trying to fix herself through other than therapy," Erika said.

"Huh," I said, recognizing that I was saying that a lot lately.

"As she told me, she was sitting around, bored and bemoaning her life, when she decided that the best way to get over one man was to involve herself with another."

"That's not wrong depending on the man you choose," I said.

"'Depending on the man you choose.' You said it," Erika said.

"I'm guessing that her new man was another mistake."

"You might say that. You might very well say that. Have a look," Erika said.

Erika pulled a manila envelope from the night table and tossed it to me. Inside were four 5X7 photos of Pamela, naked from the waist up. There were bruises on her face, neck, arms, and breasts.

"What happened?" I asked.

"A guy she met on Tinder. Claimed to be a recently divorced architect with a young daughter. He said that he lived locally and was seeking a serious relationship. She met him in town and they drove to his estate. It turned out not to be his but one where the owner was away and which he *borrowed*."

I looked again at the pictures.

"He was serious, all right," I said.

"She escaped while he was in the bathroom. Once outside and a distance away, she phoned me and I picked her up."

"Are the police involved?" I asked.

"She won't press charges. She insists that it would be political dynamite and destroy her father's career."

"What now?" I asked.

"Well, she can't stay here. My dad threw her out and put her up in a hotel. One of Vladimir's bodyguards is living with her just in case. Her father pulled strings in Washington and arranged for an arrest warrant for assault and stalking to be issued for her husband. If found, he'll be jailed to give him a lesson before being deported. I arranged her appointment with my therapist. I feel sorry for her but can't do any more. It's up to her," Erika said.

"You're right, we've done our best. The rest is up to her," I said.

Chapter 109

Returning home means becoming a child and I quickly fell into this pattern. Once again, I was an older sister, a younger sister, and my parents' dependent.

Little had changed during my absence. My oldest sister, Melody, was still having her dating disasters. Her latest began at Starbucks during a break from my father's office. She was working there as a para-legal until beginning law school.

"He was great looking and *really* well-dressed, like a TV anchor. I assumed that he worked for a hedge fund downtown and that turned out to be true. He was single and had just moved to Greenwich. He said that he was beginning work the following week and that his company had put him up at the Delamar until he gets an apartment," Melody said.

The Delamar is Greenwich's luxury hotel with superb service and gorgeous waterfront views. His company must think a lot of him, I thought.

"When are you seeing him again?" I asked.

"*Never!*" Melody exclaimed, with a laugh.

"*Huh?*

This was the third recent time that I had said this and I made a mental note to break myself of this appalling speech habit.

"He also does other work."

"Many people have a side business," I said.

"It's not one that you'd want to be associated with. He apologized for being a bit frazzled. He said that he had arrived early that morning on a flight from Los Angeles smuggling a vitamin container stuffed with Molly in his carry-on. He was flying back tonight and would return the next day.

"While listening I'm saying to myself, 'I can't date a drug smuggler.' So I chugged my drink and said that I had to get back to work. His jaw dropped a bit and he asked when we could get together again. I told him to call me and was out the door before he could remember that he didn't have my last name or number. Some you win and some you lose."

We both laughed. What she had said seemed as good a description as any of the dating life. The video game that fifteen-year-old Melanie was playing, and what my baby sister, Claudine, wore, also brought me back to reality.

Chapter 110

Randy, who had once been a videogame freak, explained them to me.

"Basically, videogames are for losers. The games demand that players fail repeatedly. They make you angry and frustrated which is what gamers call *fun*. But playing them teaches you something important too: that if you keep trying and don't give up, you'll eventually win. This is a valuable lesson at many times their price."

The game which captivated Melanie was a Japanese world-wide hit called *Dark Souls*. It is one of the current *masocore* games, this made-up-word being a combination of *masochist* and *hard-core*. The game has few instructions and punishes you. If killed, you are forced to retrace your steps and defeat previously beaten foes. Death is made to feel like the player's fault and not the game's.

Its latest version, *Dark Souls III,* begins with the player standing alone inside a nearly silent cemetery. With no music and little dialogue, they must attack the lurking undead creatures. Bloodstains show where the earlier players had died and signals that you are unlikely to survive.

To defeat these creatures, players must collaborate and share advice. "These games teach determination, flexibility, and the endurance to learn from your mistakes," Randy summarized.

As he explained, his hand had slipped under my bra to gain a different lesson. I removed it gently, feeling upset and wanting to talk. This is another message to be gained from playing videogames: that it's sometimes time to quit.

Later, passing the open door of eight-year-old Claudine's bedroom, I stepped in to chat. She was reading yet another Nancy Drew mystery. She had probably read twenty since being adopted into our family three years earlier. When she looked up, I remarked on her new over-sized square watch.

"Daddy got it for me. It's a tracking device," she said.

I smiled like an idiot and quickly left the room to seek my father.

Chapter 111

My father was seated in his favored La-Z-Boy recliner in his home-office. He looked up from his reading when I came into the room. I didn't bother giving him a kiss or even a hello before speaking.

"What's with Claudine's tracking device?" I immediately asked.

My distress was obvious.

"Have a seat," my father said, calmly.

I sat primly on the sofa, trying to control my anger. A moment later I realized that this feeling had nothing to do with Claudine. My father answered me directly.

"It's almost certainly unneeded, just for the sake of caution. Claudine's problem when she came to live with us has risen from the dead. We heard two days ago that her kidnapper had escaped from prison. It's far away, in New Mexico, but your mother worries. The tracking device is to reassure her. The kidnapper would no interest in Claudine after he was sentenced, and his gang was rounded up too."

"Oh," I said calmly, having regained composure.

"You seem upset," my father said, after several moments of silence.

I nodded, sprawled out, closed my eyes, and leaned back into the sofa.

"Bad trip?" he inquired.

"No. It was stressful but things turned out fine. I was even appointed a Deputy Sheriff. I now have the power to carry a gun and make arrests. After being called to active duty, that is."

"I don't believe it!" my dad exclaimed, and I grinned like an idiot.

"Do you want to tell me how it happened?" he asked.

"It's not a big story. Vladimir's new employee, Cody, is a retired Texas official and a friend of Austin's sheriff. Cody thought that I'd like it and I did. Want to see my badge?" I asked, still grinning, having become a bit giddy.

Without waiting for his answer, I opened my wallet and flashed the badge. Though realizing that this was childish since the badge had no meaning outside of Texas, I had kept it clipped in my wallet like the FBI agents in movies. It was ready to flash at a moment's notice and I couldn't wait to do it before my sisters.

"That *is* impressive," my dad said.

Then, after a pause, he asked, "Now, what's *really* bothering you?"

Chapter 112

My father was correct. I hadn't been OK since leaving Texas and discovering Claudine's tracking device had nothing to do with it. Sometimes, not always but sometimes, parents do know you better than you know yourself.

"I'm not sure what it is. Maybe going to Berlin for a few months," I said.

"And without Randy," my father said.

Now is the time to tell him, I thought.

"No, he insists that he's coming with me no matter what his parents say. If they object, he'll move out, leave college, and get a job to support us."

My father spoke slowly, in a lawyerly tone.

"I wouldn't think that would be necessary. His father is a bit rigid but he wouldn't push Randy from the family. Still, it *will be* a shock to your mother when she learns. Do you plan to marry?"

I shook my head.

"Neither of us is ready for that. I just don't want us apart."

My father looked at me perceptively.

"And...?" he asked.

"I'm not sure and that's probably what's bothering me. I *pressured him* to come with me and he gave in. It might not have been a good idea. Neither of us has dated anyone else, except for ..." I said.

Randy's cheating was still on my mind. Had it reflected simple drunkenness? Or his desire for a new girlfriend and explore what he felt that he had missed?

I looked at my father directly. While my parents had different personalities, their marriage was successful in the eyes of their children and kids see everything.

"How did you and mom decide to marry?" I asked, before adding a more intrusive question. "Do you feel that you made the right choice?"

A sympathetic smile crept over my father's face and I knew that he would answer honestly. Though what he told me was more advice about marriage than facts about his, that was what I really wanted.

"Maybe half the problem with many people's ideas about marriage is that it is supposed to do everything: to save us, to keep us from loneliness, to do our laundry, and more. And when it doesn't, we divorce.

"This behavior is based on the Hollywood fantasy of reality but the difference between movie life and life is that in movies the couple walk off into the splendid sunset while for real people the marriage just begins there.

"Thus, blinded by love and good intentions, we take the plunge and hope for the best. At first we want to be together all the time in our love nest. We sacrifice individuality for our relationship, surrendering long-held friends and interests for what neither of us wants to do.

"We try to be each other's best friend and continuous companion, bed and dining partner, and forsake all others to gain this. But we soon feel confined and less sure of who we are. Unneeded dependency, jealousy, and irrational fears of abandonment arise. Sensing the other's weaknesses, we tell each other the lies that we think our spouse wants to hear instead of what we feel and the marriage begins to end."

I sat spellbound, inhaling my father's words. Now I recognized why he was so highly respected as a lawyer: because he was a skilled counselor too.

"To summarize what is becoming a long lecture: When we marry for the wrong reason, from the belief that our mate can be our *everything*, divorce isn't far off. The problem with marriage is our expectations about it rather than marriage itself.

"There is no single correct formula for all couples. These are as different as the people themselves. Don't try to re-create your parents' marriage. Those who choose to love, honor, and obey should be able to promise each other anything they want without having to ask others what they think about it. Have I answered your questions?" my father asked.

I got up from the sofa and hugged him.

"More than I could have hoped," I said, with a big smile.

Chapter 113

Our study abroad for a semester was no simple matter. Paperwork from two schools had to completed and all permissions gained lest disaster occur. It had been impressed on Randy by his advisor, Professor Lee, what might result from even the most innocent mistake. Randy had remembered his teacher's words nearly verbatim.

"I didn't expect any surprises during the defense of my doctoral thesis at Harvard. There usually aren't. By the time the dissertation is completed, the faculty knows the student so well that his graduation is a foregone conclusion. So despite feeling anxious, I also felt confident.

"I knew more about my dissertation's topic than most of the professors there and their questions were elementary. That was until one of them asked, in a serious tone, what German company had introduced the first widely used antibiotic that won the Nobel Prize in 1939. This had nothing to do with my dissertation and I looked at him blankly.

"The professor then asked me for the name of a popular brand of aspirin and I replied, "Bayer." "Correct!" he exclaimed, and everyone smiled. His question had been the academic equivalent of a joke. But the next question nearly threw me into a panic.

"A representative from the Graduate School, is was on every committee, asked if I had gained permission to conduct my research. Luckily, before beginning it and while hanging around the department secretary's office, she had told me that Mr. Jelleby's signature on a form was required. She gave it to me and I went into his office. He was on the phone, waved me over, and I handed him the form. He scribbled his signature without interrupting his phone call. Had I not spoken with the secretary and obtained the signature, my dissertation would have been rejected. I would have had to do another thesis, which would have taken me years. Never forget that schools thrive on paperwork."

With this story in mind, the confidence that Randy and I had experienced upon returning from Austin ebbed away as we approached our colleges' bureaucracies.

Chapter 114

Contrary to our fears, neither Randy nor I were given a hard time by our schools. In fact, they were pleased that we were going because of the German university's reputation.

Humboldt University in Berlin is over two-hundred-years old. It has educated twenty-nine Nobel Prize winners. Its graduates have included the author, Heinrich Heine, and the physicists, Max Planck and Albert Einstein. The school has educated doctors, scientists, writers, and soon us. I agreed to speak about my experience there at Brooks Hall, the Barnard residence, upon my return to America.

Vladimir had promised to speed up the paperwork from his end and, considering his extensive contacts, I didn't doubt that he could. With this problem out of the way, we turned to our *really* worrisome task: Randy's talk with his parents.

He hadn't yet informed them of our plan. The courage that he exhibited in Austin had quickly evaporated and he was back to his usual nervous self. Worrying about symptoms that merely reflected anxiety, and about diseases that he was unlikely to catch: Lyme disease which is carried by a tic, since he refused to walk on grass; and the Zika virus, which was mostly a foreign affliction and only a literal handful of Americans had caught.

A person was far more likely to be run over by a dune buggy on the Greenwich beach than be bitten by a Zika carrying mosquito though, to be fair, Connecticut is a hotbed of Lyme disease. It had crippled my father for years.

Margaret in Berlin

Randy's other complaints were his usual: feeling hot or cold, having back or neck or stomach pains. None of these were ever taken seriously medically and his father is a doctor.

About the only symptom that Randy never complained of was PMS and if he weren't sure that this was only a woman's disease he would probably worry about that too, I told myself, a bit nastily.

In short, Randy, the love of my life and (hopefully) future husband, is a committed hypochondriac. Cool and logical with a computer project but rarely with real-life issues. Like the family task which began when we entered the restaurant.

Chapter 115

It was me who had suggested that we inform Randy's parents at a restaurant. There, in public, strong feelings are more likely to be checked and politeness reign. Usually.

Because I extended the invitation, I had insisted on paying too. Since the purpose of the meeting involved Berlin, I easily convinced myself that the meal would be a business expense and so could be paid for with the company's credit card. I wasn't yet on the payroll so this was quibbling but I didn't expect Vladimir to mind. Even the most extravagant lunch is small change to a large corporation.

Randy's father considers himself a gourmet so, despite my vegetarian leaning, I chose the elegant French restaurant, *l'escale* on Steamboat Road. You couldn't choose more French than this. Stone terra cotta tiles from Provence adorned the floors and the wood-burning fireplace was imported from a castle in France.

I tried making small talk after we were seated but this wasn't easy. I had always gotten along OK with his mother but couldn't help disliking his father who, to put it briefly, while a prized surgeon is also an opinionated bore. Ordinarily, this feeling wouldn't augur well for a marriage except when the fiancée agreed, as Randy did.

I didn't expect Randy's help at this dinner. He's a loner and seems never to have learned such basic conversational skills as asking others about themselves. I was his only friend and whatever friends we had were originally mine. But they all liked and valued him. His patient math tutoring had continued throughout high school and persisted even now for those attending nearby colleges.

Margaret in Berlin

To avoid a sticky conversation, we took a long time ordering. When Randy's mother blanched at the prices, I said, casually, "Please, it's a special occasion. Order whatever you like."

I delighted Randy's father by suggesting that he order for all. My idea received smiles from both parents. Randy and I had adopted the role of children by allowing grown-ups to make decisions for them. Or so his parents would think until our bombshell dropped.

The ordering was thoughtful and my dishes would be acceptable to most vegetarians. We each started with Kaluga Caviar on buckwheat blinis. This was followed by Plateau Royal (lobster, crab legs, and assorted seafood) for the three of them and a favorite for me, Scottish Salmon. Georgette's Salad (kale and other vegetables) was ordered for each.

Randy and I drank bottled water and wine was ordered for his parents, a half-bottle of Maison Surrenne 16 Louis XIII.

We ordered our own dessert. Randy's father chose the cheese selection with truffle honey and dried apricots for he and his wife. I chose the French Apple Tart and Randy chose the Carrot Cake. Since his parents usually shared desserts, I suggested to Randy that we share ours. Though possessive about his food, he met my eyes and got the message. Sharing desserts would be our subtle way of showing his parents that we were a couple too.

"What a wonderful meal!" Randy's father said, with a broad smile as we finished eating.

It was his last smile that evening.

Chapter 116

Randy hadn't yet raised *the* issue so I gave him a hard stare. He turned away and played with the last morsels of Carrot Cake that lay on the plate before him. I sighed and took the lead.

I had always felt unsure when addressing Randy's parents. Randy and I weren't married so calling them "mom" or "dad" wasn't appropriate. Nor were they so informal that I could comfortably call them by their names, which I now tried to remember. Were they Terrence and Jillian?

While this might sound strange, it shows how cool they were to me. Randy's mother had clung to him throughout our long relationship. This only lessened when her baby daughter was born two years earlier. I sighed again as Randy's father gave me an opening.

"Randy told us that you'll be studying in Berlin next semester. I had a chance for a stint there after my surgical residency but Jillian refused to go," he said.

"There's no place like America," Jillian added, sweetly.

As response, I smiled like an idiot. It occurred to me that, along with saying, "Huh?", I had been doing it a lot lately.

I took Randy's hand.

"Yes, we'll *both* be studying in Berlin next semester," I said.

My voice held a casual tone, as if my statement had no more significance than asking for the pepper to be passed.

"Randy attends Yale," Terrence said, with a puzzled look.

Margaret in Berlin

I stared at Randy, who looked away. "Get some balls!" I felt like screaming at him but didn't. This was the time for logic, not hysterics.

"Humboldt University has educated twenty-nine Nobel Prize winners, including Albert Einstein, and many doctors. Randy's advisor is thrilled that he'll be studying there and Barnard has asked me to speak about my experience when I return. It's a wonderful opportunity and could change his life," I said.

I dug my nails into Randy's thigh. He squirmed before nodding vigorously.

"We'll consider it!" Terrence said, as his face reddened and his wife looked away.

"No, we're not considering it. *I'm going*," Randy said forcefully.

That's my man! I thought, as I moved my hand up his thigh and squeezed again.

Chapter 117

Randy's parents were stunned by his comment and it was several moments before his father spoke.

"We'll discuss this at home," he said.

He moved his chair back from the table and began to stand.

"I won't be home tonight. We're staying be in town," Randy replied, calmly.

His statement surprised *me*. We had made no plan for the evening. These words also shocked his parents. Learning that their nineteen-year-old son is sexually active wouldn't bother many parents since it's biologically normal. But rejecting *the doctor's opinion* had.

His father sat down again.

"We have rules in *our* home," he said, ominously.

His meaning was clear: do what I say or take to the highway. We all looked toward Randy. Despite his father's forcefulness, he seemed to take charge, and I wanted to hug him. He spoke slowly, in a calm tone.

"I've been considering my future. I plan to get a Ph.D. in computer science and may get a medical degree too. But if I do, it'll be to do research. I couldn't tolerate being a practicing physician. I will be studying in Berlin with or without your approval. I would regret not having it but that won't stop me. I'm prepared to leave home."

"Yale is expensive. How would you pay for it?" Randy's father asked.

"I've considered that too. In high school, the FBI Foundation offered me a college scholarship including a leased car. I've checked and their offer is still open. The drawback is that I'd have to work for them one year for each year of school that they paid for.

"There are other possibilities. I was offered jobs in Austin. The lowest paying would start me at $150,000 a year plus stock options but taking it would mean dropping out of school. There's also an open offer from the parents of Erika's fiancée, Clarence. They have a start-up that has already gotten hedge fund money. Their company would hire me as a part-time consultant and pay for my schooling. Erika's father has invited me to live with them when I'm in town."

I saw the hurt on his parents' faces as their son's words sunk in. A joyous dinner had turned into a family crisis, though one which had long been inevitable. But I didn't want our relationship with his parents to end like this and felt that, someday, Randy would regret it too. So I patted his knee and tried to calm the atmosphere. Women are often needed to end family squabbles, I thought.

"I feel that I've been part of your family for years. Big issues shouldn't be decided quickly. Why don't we thrash things out over brunch tomorrow?" I suggested.

Jillian looked at her husband, who seemed tongue-tied.

"That's a good idea," she said, timidly.

I looked toward Randy, and then nodded.

"*Terra Ristorante Italiano* at one? The staff is good with kids so you can bring your daughter," I asked.

Jillian nodded, and I waved to the waiter for the check.

Chapter 118

We were silent after Randy's parents left and I waited for the check. Finally, I spoke.

"I didn't know that we were staying in town," I said.

"I just thought of it," Randy replied.

"It's OK now. In the future, please inform me of our plans," I said.

But I wasn't annoyed. No girlfriend would be at being acknowledged as their man's beloved to his parents.

His decision left where we would stay up to me. As usual, Randy had left me to make the practical arrangements. Well, I thought, Edison had also been a genius and his wife had probably done the same.

Since *l'escale* is on the Greenwich waterfront, I suggested that we walk to the nearby hotel, the Delamar, and Randy agreed. There, we entered arm-in-arm.

We lacked baggage but the hotel clerk supplied toiletries. I insisted on a room facing the water, away from the car park or main road. The service was all that a hedge fund investor could expect, these being their frequent clients. We were offered iced tea upon arriving and refused. We also refused the offer of a free ride around the harbor on their antique wooden boat.

Our 4th floor rooms were large and beautifully appointed, with views of the harbor. There was also a sitting area on the balcony. After locking the door, we quickly tore off our clothes, having better things to do than watch the boats below.

Margaret in Berlin

My first thought, while awaiting Randy's parents the next day, was that they would notice I was wearing the same clothes and it would be obvious how we had spent the night. But I quickly dismissed this childish notion. Considering oneself as grownup is an ongoing progression, I thought.

We had arrived ten minutes early at Terra Ristorante Italiano and sat outside. His parents walked up a few minutes late, explaining that they had difficulty finding parking. This is a common Greenwich problem.

We went inside and ordered quickly. Food was the only issue on Randy's sister's mind. She enjoyed her meal (pizza followed by ice cream) while the rest of us barely ate. But this atmosphere was more relaxed than the previous evening's. Either Jillian had worked on her husband or a night's sleep had done him good.

They accepted that Randy would study in Berlin next semester. Stopping payment of his college expenses wasn't mentioned. In fact, his father insisted on covering the cost of his stay in Berlin.

I said that wouldn't be much since the course work was free and he would be living with Vladimir, "a family friend." That Vladimir was my biological father and how I came to discover this were personal matters that I didn't plan to share.

"It went much better than I expected," Randy said, after his family had left.

"That all of our problems should be solved so easily," I said, making a small prayer.

Chapter 119

Vladimir phoned a school official, Barnard and Yale did their bit, and Randy and I were quickly admitted to Humboldt University. Considering Vladimir's contacts, this had been a foregone conclusion. Friends do favors for friends, is one of his favorite mottoes, and Vladimir had many well-placed ones.

Randy and I spent the following weeks hanging around Greenwich, saying goodbyes for what would be the longest absence of our lives. We fell back into the comfortable role of duty-less children: helping with family chores, and providing a ready ear to family members. I also got caught up on local events.

"Buddy just retired," my mother informed me, as we busily cored apples for our church's bake sale.

"*Huh?*" I replied, before again reminding myself how dumb this sounds.

"*You know*. He's owned Greenwich Taxi for decades. The town won't be the same without him," my mother said.

She handed me an article clipped from the *Greenwich Times*. When Buddy began driving, Greenwich cabs had no meters and many rides were under a dollar. He had met such celebrities as Frank Sinatra and Alice Cooper.

Sinatra was so polite that he had thanked Buddy for taking a picture with him. Cooper's wild appearance had gotten him kicked out of a Rolls-Royce showroom by a mistrusting Greenwich dealer. Cooper then bought the car at a Westchester dealership for cash, drove it to the Greenwich dealer, handed over the key, and said, "Now, you service it."

Margaret in Berlin

In a small town, business owners feel like extended family members.

I did the travel packing for both of us, assuming that European undergraduates dress about the same as in America. But I also included some clothes for business events. Though superficial, people *are* judged by what they wear.

It was while we were seated on the plane just before takeoff, that the question arose which I had been dreading.

"What happened in Nevada?" Randy asked.

Chapter 120

The stewardess' interruption, with her offer of drinks, gave me time to think. We sipped silently as Randy's question hung pregnant in the air.

I had feared it since leaving Austin. Not that I was ashamed of what had happened since the action was just. But because, as I had told Cody, Randy's personality differed from mine. Though being book-smarter than me, he lacked street-smarts. He could be perceptive about people but was often unable to use this knowledge. And he was far too sensitive and easily hurt, and could be ridden by guilt.

This guiltiness would require a psychoanalyst to explain since Randy had to be amongst the most innocent nineteen-year-olds in America. But that's how he was and I loved him, faults and all. As he loved me with mine.

So, *should I* tell him what I had viewed: the countdown, Hellfire missile liftoff and explosion. Then burning figures scrambling from the hearse until they succumbed to their appalling but deserved death.

Could I permit Randy to suffer such nightmares as I had experienced after my terrors in Greenwich and London and Tokyo?

These thoughts passed quickly through my mind, in less time than it takes to write them. In the end, I didn't tell Randy what I had seen but only its result. And, as it turned out, this had been all that he wanted. Like a child asking why their parents fight seeks only a brief, reassuring answer. Not the truth but something comforting, after asking the painful question that they knew they must.

Margaret in Berlin

In a sure, unhurried tone, I told Randy this: "There is the judgment of lawyers and the courtroom, and the justice of The Prophets and of God. Justice was done."

Then I nestled close, he embraced me, and what happened in Nevada was never spoken of again.

Chapter 121

Arriving in Berlin felt like coming home. More so than in London though, understandably, less than in Greenwich where I had lived for most of my life.

Tegel Airport was as I remembered it, still cramped and swamped with annoyed travelers. Olga picked us up and I behaved as tour guide while we traveled the route to the apartment which would be our home for months.

Though Randy and I were now "friends with benefits," I had developed the common worry of a newly married bride: fearing that her husband and her family wouldn't get along.

I didn't worry about Beauty, the only child in my Berlin family. Randy adored his baby sister and Beauty was her age. Nor did I feel that he would have a problem getting along with my step-mother. Ulrika had readily accommodated to my needs no matter how inconvenient. It was Vladimir's reaction to Randy that concerned me.

Vladimir was an unusual man. Even in his sixties and after a (mild) heart attack, his leanness was the leanness of muscular strength and his face reflected vigor and determination. Moreover, he was not an easy person to understand. Though possessing the outlook of a academic, he could have the callousness of the Borgias, that famed murderous medieval family.

Well, I'll just do my best with both men, I thought, as we entered the apartment. The silence of this usual bustling place startled me as I dropped my bags.

"Where is everyone?" I asked the housekeeper.

Margaret in Berlin

"Beauty's throat was sore. It's nothing, a little fever, but they rushed her the doctor," she said, as she led us to our rooms.

The pre-arrangement had solved another worry. An unmarried teenage couple wanting to share a room creates conflict in many families. Here, the decision had been made for us. We *were* assigned separate bedrooms, but with a communicating door between them.

Chapter 122

Vladimir, Ulrika, and Beauty arrived home an hour later. Despite Beauty's illness being minor, she was immediately sent to bed. But the usual nightly ritual of reading her a story was followed and she quickly fell asleep. Then the adults, who now included Olga, had dinner.

Olga had become almost a member of the family since her rescue years before. "Vladimir has a habit of collecting strays and particularly those that he has saved," Ulrika had once told me, in a kindly tone. She accepted Vladimir's idiosyncrasies as he tolerated hers. This is how relationships survive, I was beginning to learn.

Odd though it may seem, the six of us quickly merged to form another of today's atypical families: a father with a daughter who had grown up without him; a stepmother decades younger than the father of their child; and a once kidnapped woman whose children had been sold at birth.

Olga had become one of Vladimir's most valued employees, a bodyguard prized by the famed and wealthy. Yet despite this talent she had remained fragile, possessing a sadness that psychotherapy had been unable to heal.

Olga's children were now eight and she had vowed to find them even if never to parent them. Learning that they lived with a good family would be enough. Wrenching them from that would be a sin, she had decided.

But Olga also considered herself an avenging angel. Before she could rest, she must kill her kidnapper. He was, almost certainly, still inflicting torment on women and this must end.

Once, when Olga had spoken of her past, Vladimir had said, "The deadliest weapon is your mind. You must be a predator, but also know where to draw the moral line."

Beneath his stern exterior, Vladimir saw himself as a philosopher. But I understood for I shared this attitude. As Cody had said and I had told Randy, "There is the justice of lawyers and the courtroom, and the justice of The Prophets and of God."

Chapter 123

Studying in Germany proved more challenging than simply changing schools. For even if everyone had spoken English, student behavior was very different here.

Unexpectedly, asocial Randy became comfortable more quickly than me. Though technically an undergraduate, he was permitted to attend the University's small doctoral-level computer science program. His classes concerned computational complexity theory, which explored computer science's most difficult problems, and human-computer interaction, which tried to resolve the challenge of making computing useful to humans.

Its students, though from several nations, quickly bonded through their scientific passion and the universal language of science. But I felt adrift.

I had enrolled in the Faculty of Philosophy with classes in American Studies. It was Master's Degree level courses. The reading lists were long and began with Vernon Parrington's 1928 Pulitzer Prize winning, *Main Currents in American Thought*. The thrust of the courses was how ideas came to be considered traditionally American.

I had also enrolled in the German Language Academy. It seemed courteous to speak the language of the nation in which one lived, even if only temporarily.

Randy kept the same long hours here as in Austin. I rarely saw him during the day since our classes were on different campuses. Mine, on Campus Mitte, is the oldest of the three campuses. His classes were on Campus Nord.

Upon my return to Berlin, Vladimir had again assigned Olga as my bodyguard. She soon noticed my moodiness.

Margaret in Berlin

"Having trouble with Randy?" she asked.

"No, though I do need your help. What's the German word for *condom*?" I asked.

"They're called *kondom*. You can also ask the pharmacist for a l*umelle* though I wouldn't advise it. You'll be asking literally for a *naughty bag*. Come, we'll buy them," she said, with a laugh, as we left the student cafeteria.

Contrary to my expectation, their purchase didn't feel embarrassing. I really am growing up, I thought.

With what I hoped to be a two-month supply of condoms safely stowed in my knapsack, Olga steered us toward *Pure Origins*, a hipster café located across the street from the University's main library. There seemed few tourists despite its location close by tourist laden Friedrichstrasse.

Olga ordered a ham sandwich, a Caesar Salad, and cappuccino. I chose the Couscous Cheese Salad and an orange juice. I added New York Cheesecake to my order, to relieve homesickness. Then we ate and talked.

Chapter 124

"I'm going crazy. I can't figure out this school," I complained, while playing with the cheesecake on my plate.

"You've been to college. What's the problem?" Olga asked.

"Well, I had expected my biggest problem to be language but many people in Berlin speak English. It's the other things. I don't drink but at Barnard the students live by the motto of *work hard, play hard.* Many tackle their assignments after a blinding hangover. Here, the students drink while eating and not to get drunk.

"The workload is heavier and the few parties that Randy and I attended were held in huge cellars and filled with South Americans. That's not great when it's Germans that you want to meet.

"Most students go home on weekends, to their *real* friends, so weekends here are pretty dull. They view university as a needed stop between school and work, not years of having fun like in America."

"You're right," Olga said, nodding. "I attended the University of Minnesota for a semester. Friendships in Germany are less casual. Europeans consider American teenagers to be juvenile. Young people here tend to settle down quickly. Many in their early twenties have been in the same relationship for years, and the couples seem to remain faithful even if they don't see much of each other during the school term or attend distant schools.

"What's good here is that German men don't see women as mere sex objects. They treat them as intellectual and social equals. This sounds perfect even if I sometimes miss the flirtatiousness of American and British men."

I became calm. What Olga said had made sense of my experience here.

"Any suggestions?" I asked.

"Maybe a few. You'll have to adjust to the different culture, like speaking to a professor being more formal than in the USA. It's a plus to have a foreign accent so tell your story in German. Germans are impressed when someone speaks their language even if it's badly done so you may find making friends easier than you think. Most of all, steer clear of taboo topics like the Nazi era. The worst thing that you can call someone is a Nazi."

"I won't," I said, and raised my hand in a comical vow.

Olga smiled, and reached for the newspaper that had been left on an adjoining table. An article caught her attention and she read with increasing interest before turning to an inside page. Her face was pale and her hands shook when she looked up. It was as if she had seen a ghost.

"What is it? I asked quickly.

"*Rudolf*" she spat out.

Chapter 125

The article at the bottom of the front page was brief. Its continuation on the inside page was lengthy, and the man in the photo was named Dieter. His last name was multi-syllabic, containing the "von" and "und" of historic aristocratic German families. But the article's content was ordinary. It celebrated his promotion to a higher bureaucratic post at Humboldt University.

"He's Dieter," I said, matter-of-factly.

"No, it's Rudolf! I would recognize that face anywhere," Olga insisted.

"Even eight years later?"

"*Especially* eight years later. I've seen it nearly every night in my dreams," Olga replied.

I sat silently, neither believing nor disbelieving her.

"God is merciful. He has brought my enemy to me," Olga said.

I stared at her crazed tone and she noticed.

"I'm not crazy but I've made my vow," she said, calmly.

"To find your children," I said, though knowing that she had meant more than that.

"He must be stopped, and made to pay for his sins," Olga said.

I simply nodded. Not that I didn't believe that Rudolf/Dieter no longer deserved to exist amid the living. But were he to die, Olga might never find her children and this is what I said.

Olga nodded agreement before speaking.

"He's had the perfect arrangement. With complete access to student academic and health records, he could select perfect candidates for kidnap and insemination. Control both sperm and egg, creating babies built to order for wealthy buyers who would pay a fortune. There would be no question about the child's superiority. He could certify it, like an expert does with the origin of a work of art," Olga said.

Olga sipped her coffee during the comfortable silence that followed, amongst two people who were in agreement: Olga must find her children and Dieter must be stopped. I sensed what was coming and waited.

"I can't do it alone and your father must not be involved," Olga said.

"He would help. You're part of our family and family is very important to Russians. He always says this," I said.

"But Dieter's family is important too. Our failure would endanger Vladimir's business. I can't allow him to risk that," Olga said.

"Exactly what help would you need?" I asked.

"A computer hacker. I have friends who'll help me with the rest."

"I know a great one but he's American so you'd have to help him with the language," I said.

"Would he cost much?" Olga asked.

From my backpack, I took the bag of condoms and dropped it onto the table.

"I'll make Randy an offer that he can't refuse,' I said, with a smile.

Margaret in Berlin

Olga also smiled at this sentence from the renowned gangster movie, *The Godfather*. We left the restaurant and returned home to make plans.

Chapter 126

Another of Vladimir's sayings is that "A sound plan requires good information," and of this we had none. We knew only the basics: Dieter's name and the address of his office. Nothing of his criminal network, where he lived, or even if he had a family.

Even the most basic personal information is hard to learn in Europe which has stricter privacy laws than America. But Randy couldn't perform his hacking magic until he knew where to look!

This problem brought my thoughts back to Randy. Once again, I had volunteered his services before seeking his permission. In the past, he had willingly tutored my friends in math but hacking was a wholly different matter. Helping me with this could put him in jail, which colleges and employers frown on to put it mildly.

But Randy would accept this risk for the best possible cause, I told myself. Moreover, he had been my ally in the past though not always willingly. I had pressured him and he had given in. But this is not a good way to begin an intimate relationship, I told myself, which is what ours had been since our Austin "pre-honeymoon."

Another dilemma was whether Olga and I should tell Vladimir. If things went south, even without his involvement, his company's sterling reputation would suffer maybe irreparably. I was the daughter of the company's senior partner and Olga was his employee.

No, I would seek Vladimir's blessing, I promised myself, nodding my head as a dutiful daughter would. This act came sooner than I had expected.

Vladimir and I had been going over the business' organizational chart in my training for a managerial role. Suddenly, he leaned back and gave me his *don't mess with me* stare.

"What are you and Olga up to?" he asked, firmly.

I gave him my most innocent look before confessing.

"How did you know?" I asked.

"A general who doesn't keep track of his soldiers has many dead to account for. I've heard that Olga has been contacting former employees for help and noticed your whispered conversations."

"I was waiting for the right time to tell you," I said, contritely.

"That would have been at its beginning. Tell me now," Vladimir ordered.

So I did.

Chapter 127

Vladimir listened closely, saying nothing. Once he absent-mindedly reached for a cigarette before catching himself. He had stopped smoking several years before when Ulrika became pregnant. Old habits die hard, I thought.

Telling my story didn't take long. Vladimir already knew of Olga's kidnapping and vow of vengeance. But, along with me and the few others who she had shared this with, he hadn't expected this to occur. Successful criminals remain well-hidden or they don't survive.

By now, Dieter could have retired from his criminal enterprise or sold it. Perhaps simply identifying victims to kidnappers but not otherwise soiling his hands. Maybe even expanding his family's aristocratic heritage by marrying a woman with another impressive, multi-syllabic name

"It's a risky operation. Could Olga be persuaded against it?" Vladimir asked.

"Dieter sold her sons. Could you have been stopped from finding *me*?" I answered indirectly, in a soft tone.

Vladimir nodded agreement.

"We must help her," he said.

"She doesn't want the company involved, in case things go badly."

Vladimir nodded again.

"Then you both must be careful that they don't," he said.

As I nodded agreement, a knock sounded on the door. Without waiting for a reply, the housekeeper entered the room. She was accompanied by a man who I didn't know. He was dressed in military uniform and his gray hair was cut short in the soldierly style. He was huge, about six foot five inches, and built like the proverbial tank.

Vladimir rose and they embraced and spoke rapidly in Russian.

Vladimir turned toward me.

"I'll introduce you at tea," he said.

I got his meaning and left the room.

After the door closed behind us, I turned to the housekeeper. She seemed to know every visitor.

"Who is that man?" I asked.

The housekeeper hesitated before answering, and gave me a funny look.

"He's a Russian general, your father's half-brother which makes him your uncle. Some people call him *Lucifer* but not to his face."

Lucifer is the historic nickname for the devil. Before turning away, the housekeeper had touched the crucifix that hung about her neck.

This is *some* family that Randy is marrying into, I thought.

Chapter 128

Tea was an entirely Russian affair. These dishes aren't among my favorites but I ate enough for politeness sake.

There was Shashlik (lamb kebab with tomato-prune sauce), Golubtsy (ground beef mixed with boiled rice and wrapped in cabbage leaves), Syrniki (a cheese-filled pancake), and Russian Cucumber and Radish Salad (thinly sliced cucumber and radishes mixed with green onions, sour cream, and dill).

And, of course, whenever Russians gather, there is the ever-present Borscht (beet soup).

I filled up on the salad, Borscht, Honey Poppy Seed Rolls, and conversation.

Our Lucifer's real name, Borya, seemed appropriate for it means *battle*. Much of the conversation concerned his latest, this time on the battleground of bureaucracy. I had already learned that these can be as poisonous as the worst of high school drama.

Despite his terrifying nickname, Borya charmed us. Beauty had sat beside him and he periodically interrupted the flow of conversation by sticking out his tongue at her, making this appear to be at her control. She reacted with peals of laughter.

His recent problems arose from the latest jockeying for power in Moscow and Borya had again wound up on top. Despite this, I sensed an underlying sadness and wondered why. Only after he left did Vladimir tell me. Two months earlier, his oldest son, a military pilot, had been captured and killed while flying over Syria.

Beneath Borya's calm façade, the hatred of terrorists burned within. His presence in Berlin was to negotiate an agreement for the Russian and German intelligence services to share information about extremist activities.

This presents a business opportunity for our company, I thought, and so did Vladimir. He nodded almost imperceptibly to Borya but I picked up the unspoken message of *now*.

Randy was pigging out on Golubtsy when Borya extended the invitation, "Your reputation as a computer genius precedes you. Would you like to meet your German counterpart?"

I already knew Randy's answer. I sometimes thought that I would inevitably lose in any conflict for his attention between computers and me. I hoped to change this attitude.

It sounded like an important meeting. A representative from the company should accompany Randy, I decided, and there would be none more suitable than me. Which is what I suggested.

Borya looked toward Vladimir.

"That's a good idea. Have Olga accompany you too," Vladimir said.

I sensed that this had been his intention all along.

Chapter 129

The main office of the Federal Intelligence Service of Germany, the Bundesnachrichtendienst or BND as it is popularly called, is in Berlin, within walking distance of the federal government building and parliament. Similar to America's National Security Agency (NSA), it acts as an early warning system to the German Government. Because it relies on the electronic surveillance of international communications, Randy's computer genius was of great interest to them.

Olga drove the four of us, more slowly than her usual custom, to our 10AM meeting at BND headquarters. We entered the complex through a gate house before a grassy knoll.

Upon arrival, our phones and Randy's small-screen laptop were seized for the duration of our visit and we were given visitor passes containing a number but no name. These were collected upon our departure.

The welcoming guide proudly exclaimed that the compound was the size of thirty-five soccer fields and contained more than five-thousand rooms. It had its own generating facility which was capable of supplying enough electricity for one-hundred-thousand homes but, more importantly, its eight-thousand computers.

Borya and Randy were quickly peeled off. Borya was taken to his meeting and Randy was introduced to four senior technicians from the BND and the Militärishcher Abschirmdienst or MAD. The MAD is German's military counter-intelligence branch.

Margaret in Berlin

Olga re-acquainted herself with BND employees that she had previously worked with while a guide took me on a tour of the main building and introduced me to two officials.

That they had taken time from their busy schedules to entertain me reflected Borya's importance and not mine. They asked about Vladimir's health, knowing of his heart attack. I said that it had been minor, he was now fully recovered and working as hard as ever. No public relations official could have spoken better.

"Give him my regards and tell him that he must come for dinner. My son misses his stories," the man named Klaus said.

He handed me his card after writing a note on its back. Then he apologized for having to leave, to attend the meeting with Borya. I glanced at the note which, surprisingly, was written in Russian. It is probably the dinner invitation, I thought.

Knowing that I was a college student, the remaining man, who had introduced himself as a deputy to the President of the BND, entertained me with the story of its most famous exploit, *Operation Eikonal*. This collaboration between the NSA and the BND was the first successful mass surveillance of European telecommunications. I listened politely and tried to appear impressed but had no real interest in the historic affair. Nor, obviously, did he in me. I was merely a hanger-on to the two important visitors. Borya noticed his deprecating attitude toward me when he re-joined us.

"Margaret is a freak of nature. She has been a master of deception operations since she was thirteen and is more Russian than American," he said angrily.

"More Russian than American?" the official asked, in a puzzled tone.

Margaret in Berlin

"Yes! She is one of the breed of Americans who can battle dirtier than their enemy. Don't be deceived by her beauty. Margaret is a street-fighter with, if I may be excused my nationalism, a big set of Russian balls. I would match her against any of you. She is Vladimir's daughter, my niece, and the blood of Catherine the Great flows in her veins."

I lowered my head in a pose of humility. As Borya spoke, he had seemed transformed back into the youth he had once been. After leaving the building, I turned toward him.

"Uncle, are we really descended from Russian royalty?" I asked.

Borya placed his huge arm about my shoulder and drew me close.

"Of course not, *dushka* (sweet, sincere girl). Our descendants were peasants. But Europeans are impressed by royal ancestry," he replied.

I had learned a new lesson, and gained another protector.

Chapter 130

Ulrika arranged a going-away party for Borya before his return to Moscow. It contained the usual Russian dishes upon which Randy again pigged out. Vladimir and Borya were completely different from his father and he seemed entranced by them. They treated him as a long-lost son and each day he seemed to be becoming more Russian.

"You don't really know them," I cautioned him, as he wolfed down his second plate of Syrniki (cheese-filled pancakes).

"*Come on*, they're sweet people," Randy replied.

I just sighed, being sure that no one had ever described either of them like that before.

The Russian Consul-General in Berlin and several of his staff had joined us and the dinner became a real Russian affair complete with three brands of vodka. Randy joined in the toasts, one of which was to him, and he was pickled when we got home. I was livid.

"It stops here. Choose drinking or me! I won't put you to bed or clean up your vomit," I swore.

I was wasting my breath. After staggering to his room, Randy had flung himself fully clothed onto the bed, half-asleep. I undressed and tucked him in, making a mental note to scream at him in the morning.

When I awoke, it wasn't with this thought but with an odd sensation on my pubis. I reached down and felt hair, the top of Randy's head.

He had spread my legs and was licking inside. I moaned and, when I grabbed his head hard, he moved up and entered me. Despite this being the best sex that we ever had, I kept my earlier mental vow.

"I won't marry an alcoholic. An occasional glass of wine is OK but never more," I said, in a calm tone.

"I'm sorry. It won't happen again. I got carried away by the flattery."

I understood. A person whose genius is being applauded can't refuse to join the toasts.

"Be careful. Flatterers always want something and you may not be prepared to give it," I said.

"I'll remember. I have a good memory," Randy said.

A jarring thought suddenly hit me. Randy's memory wasn't perfect: he hadn't remembered to wear a condom that morning!

Chapter 131

My worry about becoming pregnant disappeared under the weight of activities. When not attending classes or studying German, I was immersed in Vladimir's business. It was growing in both London and Austin. I sat-in on interviews of potential hires and he sought my opinion.

But Olga's vow was never far from my mind. She had found her kidnapper and would not let him escape. Nor could I refuse her my help, or fail to seek Randy's aid. I approached this issue with him cautiously, at the Restaurant Hackescher Hof where we had been lunching regularly.

"Olga needs your help," I said.

"Sure," Randy replied, casually.

They had become friendly over the past weeks.

"It's not that simple," I said.

Then I told him of Olga's kidnapping, about her stolen children and desire for justice. Randy was moved by my story.

"We must help her," he said.

"What you'll be doing won't be legal. It could get you jailed," I cautioned.

"You too?"

"Me too."

"Adjoining cells with conjugal rights?" Randy asked, grinning.

"Our lawyers will do their best," I replied, with a smile.

"Then what do we have to lose?" Randy asked.

An awful lot, my darling, I thought but didn't say.

Olga and I ran through several scenarios before deciding on a plan. I didn't like to think what we would be doing. Still, as Vladimir had often said, "Evil men are not dealt with by Boy Scouts."

If all went perfectly we might barely avoid disaster. But if more help were needed, we had only one place to turn. Perhaps God has sent Borya into our lives to aid with this mission, I told myself, for even Lucifer might shudder at Dieter's evil.

Chapter 132

In order to succeed, our plan had three requirements: that we locate Dieter's computer holding his files; that we gain control of them to find Olga's sons; and that his crimes end.

I would have settled for the first two but this wasn't an option for Olga. In every nation, expensive lawyers and politics distort the course of justice. Her kidnapping had occurred years before and it was likely that no evidence of Dieter's crime still existed. She would render *her* sentence on him, she vowed, and who could fault her. But great care was needed since our arrest wasn't part of our plan.

Because Randy's class schedule was flexible and he wasn't known to Dieter, we relied on him to study Dieter's movements. Using a rented BMW, he studied the local streets and became familiar with the autobahn. I rented a two-bedroom apartment in East Berlin, at Rosenthaler Platz between Mitte and Prenzlauer Berg.

The apartment was completely equipped and included a washing machine, a dishwasher, and a TV with DVD-player. I smiled and told the owner that my fiancée would love the apartment too. We were Australian and would use the apartment as a base from which to explore Europe before our marriage in four months.

Olga had stolen an Australian tourist's passport and substituted my photo for theirs. With my black wig, dramatic makeup and distinctive eyeglasses, even my parents wouldn't have recognized me.

Our plan was simple, as the most successful ones are. After Randy located Dieter's computer, I would steal it, Randy would crack the password, and the location of Olga's children would be learned. Randy raised the problem that troubled me most.

"What if I can't crack the password?" he asked.

"Then we turn to Plan B," Olga said, and I shuddered.

Though Plan B was mine, I didn't like it at all.

Chapter 133

By the time that they've reached high school, every teenager knows that even the soundest plan can fail. Add things like kidnapping and hacking and matters get complex. As the days passed I felt increasingly like a bicyclist riding down a steep hill without brakes.

My costume would have aroused any pimp's admiration. The sweater was V-neck and tight, the skirt ended two inches below my crotch, and the long red boots approached my knees.

I had seen photos of Dieter and knew his schedule. Dropping my books and batting my eyes created his hoped-for reaction: an invitation for a drink. The bar was cozy and, though my earlier speech had shown innocence, I invited him to the rented apartment for dinner.

There, the wine containing Rohypnol, the date rape drug, did its part. Olga came out from the second bedroom to help me strip off Dieter's clothes and bind him with duct tape. Then I drove home, where Randy waited for Dieter's laptop. Randy had noted that it never left Dieter's presence.

I then returned to the rented apartment, to help with what further action was needed. We waited silently as Dieter dozed. I tried to study but my mind skipped over the pages. Olga's blank stare at Dieter frightened me more than would her malicious gaze.

Randy phoned four hours later. He had been unable to crack the laptop's password. Our need for Plan B had arrived.

I shuddered at the prospect of engaging in torture. But, I asked myself, wasn't I being two-faced? In the past, I had been involved with worse. Pain would be preferred to death by most people.

Yet though figuring in those events, I hadn't *direct* involvement, I reminded myself. Maybe Borya could provide those who would though I had hoped that his help wouldn't be necessary. One need be careful to whom one owes favors.

Randy's inability to crack the password had sent us onto an unmapped path. Another came after hearing the Taylor Swift ringtone, *I Knew You Were Trouble*, on my phone. I had forgotten to shut it off.

Chapter 134

The phone's screen indicated that the call was from Greenwich. I immediately feared that my father's Lyme disease had relapsed but it wasn't that.

"Is this a bad time?" my fifteen-year-old sister, Melanie, asked.

"No, it's OK," I lied. "What's up?"

"I hate to bother you."

"No, it's fine. Is everyone OK?" I asked.

"Oh, dad's OK. He's working hard but loves it though mom worries. It's about a girl at school," Melanie said.

"What's going on?"

"I really don't know. I've never had a problem with bullies but all of a sudden this girl goes out of her way to be mean to me."

"Has she put her hands on you or written anything online?" I asked.

"No, it's nothing like that. She's just being rude and nasty."

"Ignore her. It might be jealousy, she believing that her boyfriend is interested in you or something like that. Your beauty probably scares many girls and makes boys tongue-tied too," I said, feeling that a compliment is never out of place.

"Oh, *you*," Melanie said, happily. "How is school? When are you coming home?"

"Everything's great. I'll be home in two months with presents for all," I replied.

"You're the *greatest*!"

"So are you! I have to go. Stay well," I said, and hung up.

At that moment, Olga entered the room.

"Dieter is waking up," she said.

She handed me the attaché case that I had brought. Olga's rage had aroused many unpleasant ideas to gain Dieter's cooperation. One was to chop off his fingers and toes, thus giving him twenty chances to change his mind. Then, if this failed, to begin with circumcision before removing other body parts. When I objected, Olga asked, angrily, "Well, what's your plan?"

The tools needed for my plan were contained in the case. If Dieter's cooperation were more quickly gained through fear than pain, what we did should accomplish this. Or so I hoped.

Chapter 135

After becoming fully awake, Dieter stared at us in astonishment as I had hoped that he would. There was only one light on in the darkened room. It was not the breezy, sexy girl who faced him but two monsters.

Olga and I were clothed in black from our caps to our riveted jackets, studded belts, and heavy boots. Our makeup was extreme: black eyeliner and purple lipstick. Our jewelry could have come from a satanic movie.

My voice was soft and deliberate, in a take-charge manner to emphasize that we held all of the cards. I held a Taser by my side but it was Olga's scalpel that Dieter fixated on.

"Whether you live or die is of no interest to us. Your evil deeds have forfeited your right to live. But killing you might create problems so I will give you one chance. No more, just one. Do you recognize the woman by my side?"

Dieter shook his head. He seemed paralyzed with fear. Things were going well.

"Eight years ago you kidnapped, had her inseminated, and then sold her children. If I leave this room, what do you think she will do to you? I doubt that even your twisted mind can conceive what she has thought up?" I asked calmly, not really expecting an answer to my rhetorical question.

"I have convinced her that revenge would be wasteful so long as she can satisfy herself that her children are living with a good family. For this, we require access to the files on your laptop," I said.

Margaret in Berlin

At this point, apparently casually, I switched on the Taser in my hand. The glow of its "Fully Charged" indicator seemed to illuminate the room.

"You have one chance," I repeated. "What is the password?"

Dieter's eyes seemed transfixed by a vision of terror.

"How do I know you won't kill me after I tell you?" he managed to screech.

"That's a reasonable question," I answered, in a thoughtful tone. "Killing you and having to dispose of your body would *complicate* matters. The police would become involved and while what we're doing is moral, it certainly isn't legal though being applauded by many after learning what you've done. You also have our promise that we won't inform the police of your crimes, and will even return your laptop shortly.

"Once we have the information that we require, you'll be free to leave. I'll cut the duct tape nearly through with a knife beside you to free yourself. Or, if you like, you can stay and watch TV. There's no hurry. The apartment is rented for a month."

I felt that ending my spiel on a casual tone would convince him, and it did.

The laptop's password wasn't a word or a word-number-symbol combination. It was a pass-phrase which computer experts consider unbreakable. Randy couldn't have cracked it no matter how long he tried.

"I'm in and the files are a treasure trove," Randy exclaimed excitedly, after I phoned the pass-phrase to him. "They hold all of the children's dates of birth, their buyers, and the fees that were paid. There's also correspondence between him and the crime gang to which he sold his business and now sells information. They're in Hamburg."

I motioned for Olga to join me in the other room so we could speak freely.

"We can locate your children," I said.

Olga nodded, without expression. It was several moments before she spoke.

"I don't like him getting away scot-free. Despite the pain that he caused so many, he goes on to live a comfortable life with his pricey watch," she said.

Dieter wore a Marine Royale Breguet, a marine chronometer. It is so reliable underwater that scuba divers use it to warn themselves to surface before their air supply runs out. Vladimir wore one though he didn't scuba dive. His watch was for show. It cost forty-six-thousand dollars. Corporate officials must appear prosperous, Vladimir insisted.

"It won't be like that," I said.

Olga smiled when she learned my plan C. She actually smiled.

Chapter 136

"Dieter sold twenty-four babies over twelve years. Olga had the only twins," Randy told us two hours later.

We met at the Restaurant Hackescher Hof. It had taken time for Olga and me to clean our fingerprints from the apartment, wash off makeup, and change our clothes to look normal enough for a sober German eatery.

"That's twenty-three women he's kidnapped. How much did the buyers pay?" Olga asked.

"In dollars, between two-hundred and five-hundred thousand. His price increased over the years," Randy said.

"His business had a huge demand and quality product: babies with certified great DNA," I said.

"So the buyers believed but the science of heredity isn't so simple. There can be no assurance," Randy corrected.

Neither of us responded. On computer and science matters, Randy was our acknowledged expert. Olga looked at me with her unspoken question.

"I promised Dieter that we wouldn't inform the police but he won't go free. I said nothing about not publicizing his confession," I explained.

"His confession?" Olga asked, in a puzzled tone.

"Yes. The one that I plan to write. And, to make his fantastic story believable, his files will be enclosed with it."

I turned toward Randy.

"Can you hide a tracking device on his laptop, one that broadcasts his location to you when he goes online?" I asked.

"A piece of cake," Randy replied.

"Do it, my darling. Then thoroughly clean your fingerprints from it and mail it to his office."

"Which is the most reputable German magazine? One that takes care not to injure innocent parties by revealing their identity?" I asked Olga.

"*Der Spiegel*," she replied without hesitation. "It's a weekly, published on Saturday and noted for its investigative reporting. It's one of Europe's most influential magazines."

"*Der Spiegel*, it is," I said.

As they snacked on strudel and Kaiserschmarrn (a fluffy, shredded pancake), I wrote energetically.

Chapter 137

It was while writing Dieter's "confession" that I had another idea. But it wasn't one that I wanted Olga to hear. She left a few minutes later, after receiving a call from Vladimir. He had originally assigned her as my bodyguard-guide to Berlin. Now that he considered these duties to be no longer needed, he planned to reassign her. I hoped that her new duty would be local. I would miss our girl-chats.

When Olga was gone, I turned toward Randy. He was finishing his third piece of strudel. Over the past weeks I had been slow to supervise what he ate but no more. Other boys would have objected but my overseeing behavior had begun years before, soon after we began dating. Then, he would ignore his mother's demand that he gets a haircut but not mine. As a somewhat genius, he seemed to recognize his need for help with practical matters.

I explained my plan slowly.

"Randy," I said, in a deliberate tone.

He looked up from his plate.

"The American legal tradition is for an injured person to gain payment for their suffering. Isn't that correct?" I asked.

"Sure," he replied.

"Olga was badly hurt by Dieter. He destroyed her life and she grieves for her sons. Did you find banking records on his laptop?"

Randy's eyes lit up and a smile curled his lips. He understood where I was going.

"Yes, he does all of his banking on line. I could access his IDs and passwords. His total balance, on all of his accounts, is nineteen-million Euros, twenty-one-million dollars at the current conversion rate."

"That's far more than could have been made from his baby-selling business. How did he get so much?" I asked.

"From his other dealings. Mostly, scheduling tours to Thailand for men interested in having sex with kids, and engaging in blackmail on the side."

"It wouldn't be just for him to flee into a well-heeled retirement while Olga continues suffering, would it?" I asked.

"Absolutely not!"

"Could you wire money from his bank accounts to others that I'll set up?" I asked.

"A piece of cake. I spent an entire day at the Austin conference learning the latest money-laundering techniques. To combat it, of course," Randy said.

We both smiled and I didn't object when he reached for a fourth piece of strudel.

Chapter 138

Among the lessons that Vladimir gave me was one on internet banking. Opening accounts proved surprisingly easy. Using his personal contacts and an encrypted connection, I opened nine bank accounts: three each in Macao, Luxembourg, and Belize. Hours later, I wired into them the bulk of Dieter's assets from his banks. Everything went smoothly and I received confirmation of my nine deposits within minutes.

I then wired most of this money into other bank accounts that I had opened. The money's final destinations were four accounts, two banks in Switzerland and two in Hong Kong. The titles on the accounts were four fictitious corporations with proper sounding names that had been set up by a lawyer in Hong Kong. Only I was permitted access to the money.

I left Dieter with two-hundred-thousand Euros for escape money. I intended for my Plan C to ensure that he not be on the run for long.

"We're rich!" Randy said, yawning.

It was 3:25AM and we had been up nearly two nights, taking advantage of the international time zones to make transactions.

"We'll always be rich so long as we have each other, my darling. The money will be our family's cushion, and help others that we love. I've decided that Olga is entitled to three-million Euros for her pain."

Randy smiled, and nodded agreement.

Another of Vladimir's pieces of advice is that no matter how good a plan is, something can go wrong. What now went wrong was that my writing of Rudolf's phony confession wasn't working. I played with the wording for hours but it never sounded honest. Psychopaths like Dieter "find God" only when confronting a parole board. This idea had been bad from its start.

I changed course. From Dieter's E-mails I learned that he owed four-million Euro to "Hans." This would be a fine motive to inform on him. I hoped that the editor of *Der Spiegel* would agree.

Randy had placed a hidden program on Dieter's laptop. When he opened Internet Explorer, he would really be opening a different program that was invisible to him. It looked and functioned like Explorer but was a mirror image located on a server in Finland.

This program enabled Randy's "hostile takeover" of Dieter's machine. When Dieter booted up his laptop, he would be working not on his machine but on our server. "His computer will run slower but not so much that he'll notice," Randy had told me.

Whenever Rudolf pressed a key on his computer, Randy could see this on *his*. Thus, Randy hid from Dieter the changes that we made in his banking accounts. Randy also held back the confirmatory E-mails from these banks about our fraudulent transactions.

"You *are* a genius!" I burst out, after he explained.

"Maybe a little but the smartest thing that I ever did was to choose you," he replied.

"I always thought that it was me who chose you," I said, with a hint of feigned annoyance.

I pushed him onto the bed.

"Lean back and relax. I'll take care of everything," I said.

There was no more talking that night.

Chapter 139

Two days later, Vladimir looked up expectantly as I arrived for breakfast in the dining room. We usually ate together early, before everyone else. He would then leave for his office while I went to my German tutor's apartment for my daily lesson.

"Olga said that things went well," he said.

"They couldn't have gone better," I replied.

"Good," he said, and changed the subject.

Just as my lawyer-father in Greenwich, there were some things that Vladimir preferred not knowing. Having *plausible deniability*, lawyers call it.

"She's looking for you," Vladimir said, before kissing me on the forehead and leaving.

Olga was still in bed when I told her.

"I've opened a numbered bank account for you in Hong Kong. It contains three million Euro, as payment from Dieter for your suffering," I said.

I handed her a sheet of paper containing instructions for retrieving the money.

"It'll allow you to start over. You can continue working for Vladimir or battle in court for your children. Vladimir knows nothing of my action and it must remain this way," I said.

Olga's mouth gaped open but she said nothing and just stared.

Margaret in Berlin

"Aren't you going to say anything?" I asked, with a broad smile.

Olga didn't. She just leapt from the bed and hugged me.

The computer files that *Der Spiegel* anonymously received were accompanied by a cryptic note: "Evil must be outed." I left it to the editor's imagination to interpret. Then we waited.

The public storm broke three weeks later. The magazine's banner headline lay above a photograph of Dieter speaking with a busty girl at Humboldt University: "University Official Involved in Kidnappings and Sex Tourism." Within its covers were more photos: Dieter leaving the University, getting into his car, and hiding his face from reporters at his family's ancestral home.

The reporters had done a good job. The story covered thirteen pages and the magazine's online edition held most of the files that they received with the victim's identifying information being removed.

Randy and I had been exploring restaurants close by school. As we sat in the Weihenstephaner bistro, reading the article online, I felt a sense of satisfaction for how things had turned out.

"I was thinking of Olga," I said.

"Yes?"

Randy looked up from his laptop.

"I'm glad that we sent her the money. The least that you can do for some people in this stupid brawling world is to give them a sense of comfort before their end comes," I said.

Randy's response wasn't what I had expected. He looked into my eyes and took my hand.

"I don't deserve you. You're such a good woman," he said.

Chapter 140

Despite all of Germany's problems, from the expanding Volkswagen emissions lawsuits to terrorism and widespread flooding, Dieter's disappearance became center stage. The Berlin Landespolizei (police) issued a warrant for his arrest and Interpol was notified.

Public interest was unquenchable. Everybody wondered about the informer. Theories of their identity included a guilt-ridden lawyer, a dissatisfied accomplice, and even a drug-addicted family member. An abandoned girlfriend was the most popular guess.

Dieter was reported to have been seen in Zurich, London, Capetown, and points between. As proof of his identity, a photo of a white man wearing sunglasses, slacks, and a sport jacket, walking along a Bermuda beach, was submitted. Though he could not be identified, local newspaper reporters unsuccessfully tried to find him. Over subsequent weeks, interest in this case diminished with news of the latest terrorist attack.

Meanwhile, the tracker that Randy had placed on Dieter's laptop followed his travels. We read his increasingly frantic correspondence as he sought explanation from his banks about his missing funds.

Dieter was informed that only *he* could make withdrawals. His presence at the bank was not required. It was enough for him to present a series of clearing codes to transfer the money to another bank. The clearing codes had been correct and the banks were blameless in these transactions.

A month later, using a throwaway phone, I called the Bremen partner who was owed money.

Using a voice-altering gadget borrowed from Vladimir's warehouse, nineteen-year-old Margaret became forty-year-old Hulk.

"Hey, fucker, wanna know where Dieter is?" I asked.

"Who is this?"

"Your mother's pimp. Are you interested?"

"Yes."

I told him. Three days later, midway through the evening TV news, came the bulletin of Dieter's badly beaten body being discovered in Lisbon. It was probably a robbery gone bad, the police suggested.

I thought of Olga and the other women who had been violated. Dieter's debt was paid, insofar as it could. The TV blared on as I left the room to get a glass of juice.

Chapter 141

The ending of the school term meant our leaving Berlin. Things had calmed down. Following Dieter's death, he was no longer considered newsworthy and he passed from my mind too. Olga had located her children in Manhattan and planned to check on their welfare. Knowing New York City, I agreed to accompany her when she came.

Randy was offered admission into Humboldt University's doctoral program even without a college degree and the Bundesnachrichtendienst, the Federal Intelligence Service of Germany, offered to pay for his educational expenses and guaranteed him a job at its completion. This was what the FBI had offered him six years earlier when they became aware of his computing talent.

Randy was tempted to stay, as was I. We had come to love Berlin and would miss Vladimir and Ulrika and Beauty. But we had family in America and are, at heart, American.

That afternoon, I was alone with Ulrika and Beauty. Vladimir was at a business meeting and Randy was presenting a paper at the University.

"Are you all right?" Ulrika asked me suddenly.

I had been playing a board game with Beauty and Ulrika's question came out of the blue. So I did what people often do when asked a puzzling question: ask a question in return.

"Why do you ask?"

"Well," Ulrika began slowly, "You seem tired and have been using the bathroom often. Maybe you should see a doctor."

I considered what she said. I didn't like seeing doctors and, apart from recommended vaccinations, rarely did. My near miraculous childhood recovery, from a here-to-fore believed fatal illness, had caused me to avoid them thereafter. My fear wasn't nearly as bad as Randy's but in this respect we made a good couple. Still, what Ulrika had said made sense.

"Maybe I should. I've been tired lately and pee a lot more. This morning I was nauseous too," I said.

Ulrika looked at me closely and a smile spread across her face.

"What?" I asked.

"Can you watch Beauty for a few minutes? I have to go out," Ulrika said, getting up.

"Sure."

"I'm winning," Beauty warned.

Ulrika returned a half-hour later and handed me the small package that she held.

"The indicator is in German: *Schwanger, Nicht Schwanger,*" Ulrika said.

I had already learned these German words. They meant *Pregnant, Not Pregnant.*

Chapter 142

Randy and I are a quiet couple. We felt no need for a going-away party but Ulrika insisted on holding it.

"Life is hard so celebrations are important," she said.

I had expected this party to be at home with just family and a few friends attending. Instead, it mushroomed into one of Vladimir's business affairs and was held at the ballroom of a local hotel.

Most of the guests came from the German intelligence services and the Russian Consulate. I had thought that I knew Vladimir well but this was a mistake as I learned after speaking with several of them.

Some guests loved him and others, I knew, were loved by him. Yet a few of them seemed to dislike him though whether from sound reason or envy I didn't learn.

Vladimir is complex. His integrity is undisputed and his handshake is enough to seal an agreement. He is trustworthy to acquaintances and loyal to friends. His generosity is never questioned.

He could be warm and charming but also petty. He could be cruel or kind. He had no interest in music, had to be dragged to a museum, and avoided driving a car. I also sensed that he would have liked to skip this party.

Except for Borya, few of the guests were familiar to me. He had flown from Moscow, accompanied by his third trophy wife. Tanya was pretty and thirty years younger than him.

She greeted me warmly while her much younger sister, Marta, a drop-dead gorgeous girl of about my age, zeroed in on Randy.

"I've heard *so much* about you," she breathed into his face, in virtually unaccented English.

Randy seemed hypnotized by her beauty as she hugged and then kissed him on both cheeks in the European style. Her barely contained breasts and micro-skirt made him unsure where to put his hands. Dealing with social events and girls aren't among Randy's strengths.

I stared at Marta with daggers until her sister guided me away and whispered.

"I was born with the brains and she with the beauty. You have nothing to fear. Her fiancée would beat her if she misbehaved. She is like this with all attractive men. Consider her behavior a compliment to your taste."

I calmed down and looked toward Borya.

"Does he...?" I asked, not wanting to complete the sentence.

"No. He's told me that I'm his final wife and is like a puppy. Besides, my father would have him killed if he ever hit me," Tanya said.

I smiled and decided that marrying an American man is safest. My concern was also aroused by Borya's long conversation with Randy. He later explained.

"Borya invited me to study in Moscow. He said that the government would pay for everything and give me an apartment too. After graduation, I would be offered a job at three times the salary of any other proposal. He said that Moscow summers are not to be missed."

"Did you ask him about Moscow winters?" I asked, under my breath.

"What?"

"Nothing. What did you say?" I asked.

"That we would consider it but just now we miss our families in America. He likes you a lot and wants to hire you. He'll pay you *a lot* of money," Randy said.

"Randy, I didn't study in Europe only to return to America as a Russian spy," I said, in a deliberate tone.

"Oh, I'm sure he didn't mean *that*," Randy said, a bit shocked.

His innocence was touching. I dropped the subject, draped a possessive arm about him, and moved closer.

"We'll talk about it on the plane," I said.

But we never did for there was something far more important that we had to discuss. And, while seated on the plane awaiting takeoff, Randy gave me the perfect opening.

"I'm glad that you pressured me to study in Europe. I never liked to travel. I was afraid of getting sick or being hurt but nothing like that happened. We left America in good health and the two of us are returning in good health," Randy said, with a big smile.

I put my arm about him, pulled him close and placed one of his hands over my belly. Then I covered it with mine.

"No, my darling, *two* of us left America but *three* of us are returning," I said softly, giving him that special look of pregnant women.

It took several moments for Randy to grasp my meaning. As he stared open-mouthed, a line from a story that I had read as a child passed through my mind: They who have once been happy have received life's promise and made a conquest of time.

www.ingramcontent.com/pod-product-compliance
Lightning Source LLC
Chambersburg PA
CBHW020250200626

46816CB00001BA/222